A Poem
For What's Her Name

Dani O'Connor

2006

Copyright© 2006 by Dani O'Connor

Spinsters Ink
P.O. Box 242
Midway, Florida 32343

All rights reserved. No part of this book may be reproduced or transmitted in any form or by any means, electronic or mechanical, including photocopying, without permission in writing from the publisher.

Printed in the United States of America on acid-free paper
First Edition

Editor: Anna Chinappi
Cover Designer: LA Callaghan
Cover Art: Otis Smudge

ISBN 1-883523-78-8

This book is dedicated to one astounding woman in particular, you know who you are. Your support, inspiration and love are the most valued things in my life. Thank you for putting up with me and my late night rants. Thank you for ignoring me as I take on the life of my characters and forget that the real world still exists. Thank you for looking the other way when I wear pajamas for three days and eat out of the cat food bowl. Thank you for teaching me the happy dance. I am blessed to have you in my life, in my heart and in our home. You have inspired me to find my true self and made it okay for me to dream—for that I am forever grateful. You are my beautiful muse. I can't imagine what I'd be without you and I hope I never find out.

Acknowledgments

To the Texans: Diana, Sherry, Susan, Erik, Misty, Sylvia, Sandra, Melanie, Patty, John, Julie H., Lori, Cindy, Jennifer, Norm, Stephani, Beth, Julie B. and Casey; and Marjolein in Amsterdam, as well as the dozens of other friends who helped me understand that being myself isn't so bad. Thank you all for making my own coming out a remarkable journey without regret.

To my mom, thank you for your advice, support and credence. Thanks also for your humor, creativity and strength. I am proud to be your kid.

Thank you, Stallion, for the opportunities and generosity. I truly appreciate all of it.

To Linda at Spinsters Ink, thank you for giving me the gift of my first publication. Thank you to Anna, the editor, for making everything better.

Thank you to all my friends and family who made me realize that a living is what you earn and a life is what you make.

About the Author

Dani O'Connor is a former teacher, starving artist and moderately successful business owner. She was born in a small Wyoming town but currently resides near Dallas with her partner, a multitude of animals and a growing collection of Converse and cowboy shirts.

Chapter One

My Internet profile read like this:

Educated MTV addict with a penchant for bad fashion and dull conversation seeks overly attractive, high maintenance, money grubbing, curious, "straight" woman for bad dates and awkward kisses. You should be prepared to use me anytime and dump me on a whim to return to your husband/boyfriend. I am into transcendental vegetation—"I think, therefore, I yam." I like long walks through airports and singing in public restrooms. I have perfect teeth and perfect feet. Everything in between is a cruel joke told by gravity. I am in a very vulnerable place in my life, so please be willing to take advantage of my insecurities and need for affection. I drink, smoke and use prescription medication. You should be prepared to overlook my chain-smoking, drug addiction and alcoholism; but feel free to complain about it every second of every date. I do not have a sense of humor and I lack patience. If I tell you that you are a flake, I am being serious. Please do not laugh at everything I say as I am sure most of the time it will go over your head. Boring tales of your job will put me to sleep. I need sleep, so please don't try to wake me. Any attempt to change my hair, clothes or habits will lead to bitter resentment and removal from my Christmas card list. You must insist on flaunting me in front of all your exes and treat me like dirt when they don't respond. More important, you must treat me like less than dirt if they do respond. Please don't invite me to the wedding; getting you back together is reward enough. I don't like intellectual conversation, so I would appreciate a woman who is not familiar with Darwin, Dorothy Parker or anyone not associated with "Cosmo magazine." I am turned on by women who call me "hun" and use alternate spellings like "kewl." If you think you can meet any or all of my criteria, I would love to hear from you. Normal, intelligent, funny, fit, attractive women need not apply; you don't exist. I might as well date the Easter Bunny.

Needless to say I only got a handful of responses. It wasn't that I was bitter, I was basically just burned out. I spent a few years in the dating scene and had some horrific experiences. I went on thirty-eight dates in ten months and not one of them led to a second date. When talking to my friends about these women, I never used first names. I referred to them by their flaws. I then made a rule—if someone has a big enough flaw to eclipse their given name, then they are not worthy of a second date.

GRANDMA GIRL arrived on our date carrying a crocheted purse and wearing starched jeans. She ordered a Cosmopolitan "because she liked the magazine." G.G. sipped on her Cosmo for three hours. I went through five beers and a whiskey sour because the bartender insisted on the latter after she met my date. Said date was currently unemployed but it was okay because she lived in her grandparent's basement and they pretty much covered all her bills. I couldn't resist asking if they gave her money for Cosmos. She tittered politely. Grandma Girl was 41 years old.

BLONDE BARBIE was not blonde, but I am pretty sure she was made of plastic. She was as dumb as a bag of hammers and not afraid to use it. She said she hated the butane smell that came from motorcycles and cigarettes. She got to travel a lot for work and bragged about flying first class to Australia on Kwanza airlines. When her car ran out of gas on the highway, she walked back and forth to the gas station fourteen times until her tank was finally full. She asked me what day of the week Thanksgiving would be on that year so she could make travel arrangements. She could never remember where she parked her car and on our date she cried all the way to the parking lot. She felt much better when I reminded her that I had driven us in my car. She did have one redeeming quality, I just never figured out what it was.

BOOBIE BABE was extremely attractive and exceptionally tall. We met at a bowling alley, which I know now is not a good place to pick up chicks. We arranged a date for the following weekend. I picked her up and had to wait fifteen minutes while she optimistically changed the sheets. We went downtown to see my favorite local band. I made the usual small talk—where are you from, do you have siblings, what do you do, any hobbies? I was given one-word answers all night—Texas, yes, post office, no hobbies. (Okay, maybe a few two-word answers). We sat in silence most of the evening. When we arrived back at her place, I asked if I could use the bathroom. The one-word response was affirmative. When I exited the bathroom, I was greeted by a topless Amazon who finally spoke, "Be careful, they're perfect." I was shocked not by the perfection of her breasts, but by the fact that she actually said four words without being questioned.

NASTY NELLIE may have been a man and I debated the possibility all night. She was a little too effeminate for a typical lesbian and her face was a little too hairless. When she handed me a drink, I stared at her hands—no hair, huge knuckles. When she crossed her legs, I looked at her ankles—no hair, fraternity tattoo. When she went to the bathroom, I noticed women coming out making whispered remarks. Eventually, I became determined to find out for sure so I kissed her in the parking lot. I couldn't tell much from the kiss—strong jaw, good breath, subtle perfume. We kissed for about five minutes before I felt the bulge grow beneath her dress. She just laughed and offered no apology for the deceit. I was strangely aroused and offer no apology for that. We did not have a second date but I set him up with one of my friends for shits and giggles.

FORGIVING FEMME was gorgeous from head to toe. She made no attempt to understand my humor. I overlooked her despicable grammar because what she lacked in subject-verb agreement she made up for in breast-hip proportion. In my mind, I rationalized the fact that we had nothing intellectually in common. I spent the entire night deciding to take it slowly and hanging on her every word, no matter how routine. I tried very hard not to cringe when she used the word "ain't." I played slightly hard to get when she tried to kiss me in the parking lot. I even asked her out for the following weekend. The morning after our first date I received an e-mail that stated: "Even tho you drink to much and smoke to much and were married too a man and dont like dogs and read to much. I think that we will make a good couple." I sent a detailed response stating that although I appreciated her overlooking all my flaws, I was dreadfully allergic to dogs and didn't think it would work out.

JEWISH JILL was adamant that I accept the fact that she was Jewish. She spent two hours telling me that it is important to keep an open mind and not judge people based on religion, political affiliation or race. I suffered through an evening of one-sided conversation then politely told her I'd call. The next morning she called to inform me that although she had a wonderful time, she just didn't think she could date a teacher who probably made less than $30,000 a year. I wanted to remind her that I was head of the department at the university, but it just seemed shallow.

ICKY ISABEL was pretty cool. She liked to piss me off and push my buttons. I appreciated a good debate and found her attractive in a "Beverly Hills 90210" sort of way. We danced and had a few drinks then headed back to her place for some wine. After we downed the entire bottle and she showed me her extensive collection of John Tesh memorabilia, I was totally ready to pass out. She offered me her bed and kissed me very seductively. Then she whispered in my ear, "I think oral sex is icky, don't you?" I explained to her that it is the basic premise of lesbian sex. She argued that there are other things that can be done. I offered that if there were no oral, why would you need a partner. She reiterated that oral is just flat out icky. I implied that maybe she has some trust issues. She told me not to put words into her mouth. I remarked that apparently that was the only thing I was going to put in her mouth. Seeing as how I was too drunk to drive home, I spent the rest of the night sleeping in the back seat of my car. To this day, the word "icky" makes me think of John Tesh.

So, after no second dates, zero multiple orgasms (or even singular ones for that matter) and utter bitterness, I finally gave up on dating. I occasionally checked the mail on my profile when I felt like being brave or more discouraged. I replied to a few who seemed remotely intriguing and explained to them that I had recently joined a nunnery and that the sisters don't like me bringing women back to the convent. They felt it was a bad habit. After a few months of mundane mail, I finally got a reply worth reading twice:

Dear Sarcastic Professor,

I am writing to inform you that if you are as bitter in real life as you seem on paper, then perhaps you don't drink, smoke and drug enough. Try upping the dosage and everyone will seem tolerable. You needn't respond to my e-mail, as you are way too old for me. I refuse to spend my life taking care of an acidic, aged asshole who thinks she is too good for everyone. I only read "Cosmo" in the waiting room of my gynecologist. I bet no woman has ever mentioned her gyno in a response to your ad. I felt it important to set myself apart from all the others. You probably don't care that I was an ambassador to Jamaica before taking a job with the CIA. I would tell you more but then I'd have to figure out what CIA actually stands for. I am sure that you are profoundly impressed that I ended that last sentence with a preposition.

I will not share further details about myself. I refuse to waste my time seducing you when I am sure that you have some sort of standard e-mail response that you send to all the lunatics. Let me guess . . . it is glib, ostentatious and contains a bad pun. You bitter elderly women are so predictable. I look forward to receiving your customary response. Perhaps I will have it framed for posterity.

Enjoy your endless search for the figment of your imagination.

Best wishes,

The Easter Bunny

I waited three days to respond and rewrote my reply six times:

Dear Ambassador Bunny,

Thank you for responding to my profile. It is so rare to find a woman who not only visits the gynecologist, but who actually knows how to spell it. I am sorry to hear that I am too old for you; perhaps you have a mother or grandmother who might like to go dancing one night. I am not sure what CIA stands for either; maybe it's Cousin In Arkansas for the white trash set. For the lesbian group, I will submit Clingy Insane Androgynous.

I appreciate your keeping your details to yourself. At my age, seduction by an intelligent woman might just give me a heart attack. I will admit that I do indeed have a standard e-mail reply that I send to be polite. Yes, you busted me, and for the record, the pun wasn't really that bad. If you should decide to share some tidbits about yourself, I will be happy to reciprocate. Please don't let my bitterness fool you. Once you get past my crusty exterior and overlook all the wrinkles, I am relatively harmless.

Take care,

Professor Predictable

She replied within minutes:

Dear Predictable,

I will not waste a lot of your time with e-mail flirtation. I know at your age it is important to get the ball rolling. Let's trade basic necessities and see who runs off to Zimbabwe first. I am a year past legal drinking age; I had two of my three heads removed shortly before prom—some say I am attractive . . . but you know how flattering moms and grandmas are. By the way, neither was interested in your dancing invitation. If your profile was correct, we live in the same zip code; however, I will be heading back to school in a few months. I am currently interning with a local firm three days a week. I spend the other four days stalking old women and harassing young children. Tonight is my stalking night, so I will be the lady in red playing pool at Splinter's.

Ball's in your court, Martina.

Billie Jean

My hands were shaking from excitement as I wrote my response.

Dearest B.J.,

You already have all my details from my profile. I hope you feel that six years is not like the Grand Canyon. As long as you know what Motown is, I think we will be okay. I will not commit to nor deny your subtle invitation; however, beware of women in glasses carrying tequila shots.

M.N.

I did not get another response, which is exactly what I was hoping for. It meant that she was confident and I loved self-assured women. I adored the fact that she was playing pool at a straight bar and didn't feel the need to arrange a meeting in the alternative triangle of our city. Splinter's was two blocks from my house and one of my favorite hangouts. I wondered if I had seen her there before. I perused my memory trying to recall all the women I had seen playing pool recently. I came up with a few faces and dismissed two out of the three. The third woman I recalled was vibrant, gregarious and gorgeous. I didn't get my hopes up though, as I am a confirmed pessimist. I couldn't decide whether I should go it alone or bring a friend with me in case I needed an escape. I decided to invite my ex-husband, which probably seems odd. He and I had the same taste in women, so I knew if he liked her, she was a keeper. Unfortunately, he was already committed to attend a charity event that night. I discharged the idea of inviting some of my other friends for fear that the lady in red might like them better than me. We confirmed pessimists have low self-esteem.

Chapter Two

Oh, what to wear, what to wear. I was not sure why I was so concerned about the impression I made on this youngster. I spent the better part of an hour changing clothes and as usual, ended up wearing the first thing I put on. I never learned that the first impulse is usually the best. I fried up a large hamburger patty knowing that I would need a strong protein base to do tequila shots on a weeknight. You know you are getting old when you do hangover prevention before you even start drinking. I ate my burger in silence and stared at the clock. Time was moving too slowly, so I decided to leave early and go to another bar first, maybe have a drink or two to loosen me up.

I walked the two blocks to a little jazz bar across the street from Splinter's. I bellied up to the counter and ordered myself a Miller Lite. The bar was pretty empty, just a few yuppie couples who had probably been there since happy hour and me. A few minutes later a stunning couple came in the door laughing and being quite friendly. They sat across from me and ordered beers. The couple seemed very familiar. He had that type of infectious smile that straight women adore. His girlfriend had that comfort about her like she could be your best friend if you got to know her. I made an attempt to eavesdrop on their conversation because I like to steal dialogue for my short stories. I couldn't hear them over the jazz. I sat watching their body language, the way they teased each other and jovially punched each other's shoulders. They both took turns glancing up at me and smiling. I returned the smiles feeling a little embarrassed that I was sitting alone. They each had one more beer, paid the tab and left arm-in-arm.

I stared awkwardly at my third beer and checked my watch. I elected to leave the beer half full and head across the street. When I asked for my tab the bartender informed me that the loud couple put my drinks on their tab. I asked if he knew them and he just shrugged. I put a few dollars on the bar for his tip hoping to get some more information. He merely smiled so I left feeling a bit confused. It seems like it took me forever to finally get to Splinter's. My cell phone rang and I spent ten minutes listening to my mother ramble. Next, a homeless guy cornered me and didn't pipe down until I gave him a five. Finally, I made it to my destination much later than I had intended.

The place was pretty crowded, so I wandered around for a few minutes. I slowly made my way to the pool table area to catch a glance of the mysterious lady in red. I didn't see her but I did see the fun couple from the jazz bar. I decided to thank them for the drinks while I waited for my Internet friend. I went up to the bar and ordered three beers then headed back to the couple. As I approached them they both started laughing and punching each other again. It occurred to me why they had seemed so familiar—they played pool here all the time. In fact, she was the gorgeous gregarious woman I had in my mind. I was a bit crushed to discover that she had a boyfriend and could not be my Easter

Bunny.

"Hey, I wanted to thank you for the beers." I handed them each a bottle.

"No problem, you seemed lonely, so we wanted to be friendly."

I didn't know what to say when I found out they had bought me pity drinks.

"No, I wasn't lonely, just killing time." I blushed.

"Do you always kill time in bars? That could be a sign of alcoholism, you know."

"No, I am supposed to meet someone and just got down here a bit early."

She leaned over the pool table and I felt my face get hot. I looked up at her date and he was grinning at me. I felt so uncomfortable, but didn't want to leave the area in case my new friend came in. I made small talk with the couple and intermittently checked the entrance for a woman in red. Every time a single woman walked in, my heart jumped. Not one of those women was in red and not one approached.

"Looks like you got stood up." The infectious smiling male remarked.

"Looks like I did." I replied as I glanced at my watch and tried not to blush.

His girlfriend returned from the bar with three shots and three beers. I decided I might as well drink my woes away and took one of the shots. She clinked glasses with me and smiled a smile that lit up the room. The three of us continued on with the small talk for another hour, nothing detailed, just heavy sarcasm and a little political discussion.

"My brother thinks you're cute." The beauty whispered and winked.

"Your brother? Oh! So is he . . . although not my type, really."

"Yeah, I figured he was a bit too straitlaced for a wild woman like yourself."

"Something like that." I winked back.

I racked up the balls for another game and took another drink. The beauty beamed at me.

"It's your break, Professor."

My heart jumped, yet I didn't miss a beat.

"No, after you, Ambassador."

I can't say that I was totally shocked to find out that she was the one I was waiting for. The conversation all night seemed to be intentionally evasive. We never exchanged names, or occupations or anything personal for that matter. We did, however, exchange tequila shots and lingering glances. I felt very comfortable with her all night. She and her brother kept looking at each other like they shared some sort of hysterical inside joke.

"So, why aren't you wearing red?" I teased.

"I realized my red shirt was at the dry cleaners and would have felt stupid e-mailing you back over something so trivial." She chewed on her fingernail.

"I never mentioned in my profile that I am a professor, you know."

"Word gets around. You see a beautiful woman at a bar, you make inquiries. Your friends told me you had a profile on that site. They offered to introduce me to you, but I wanted to see if I could win you over on my own."

"I see." I was speechless and totally euphoric.

"And did I?" She looked nervous.

"Did you what?" I asked, knowing what she meant.

"Did I win you over on my own?"

I couldn't help it. She was so adorable at that moment. She looked so nervous to hear my reply. I stared at her for a minute to keep her in anxious anticipation. I don't know whether it was the tequila, the moment or the smell of her perfume. I leaned over and kissed her on the neck. When I looked back at her face, her mouth opened slightly like she wanted to speak. Her eyes got a little watery and her face was as red as her shirt was supposed to be.

"I'm sorry," I stammered, "I shouldn't have done that so soon and in this bar."

"I have been watching you for months wondering what it would be like to feel you that close to me." Her eyes were round and looked like an ocean.

Her brother came back from the restroom and wrapped his arms around his sister. I stood there staring deep into her eyes until she finally blinked back the tears. I couldn't understand her emotional response. I felt awful, like I had scared her or reminded her of a lover who broke her heart. I rationalized that it was probably the smoke in the bar and that she was allergic. I just kept staring at her and she just kept looking wounded.

Finally her protector spoke, "What's next on the agenda, ladies?"

Neither one of us responded.

"C'mon. The night's still young and none of us has to work tomorrow."

"Actually, I have a class in the morning." I came back to reality.

She looked totally dejected and again. I felt awful. I felt the need to redeem myself.

"But tomorrow is Friday and I don't have any plans all weekend."

She grinned from ear to ear and returned her brother's embrace.

"Well then, Professor, maybe we should walk you home so I know where to pick you up tomorrow." She seemed confident. "That is, unless you want to pick me up."

"No, Ambassador, you can drive me." I realized my entendre and got flushed.

The three of us took the long way back to my house. The siblings walked with arms linked and I limped up and down the curb like an ecstatic child on her way to the toy store. When we arrived at my porch, I asked them if they wanted to come inside. They shot each other a knowing glance and both declined at the same time. The male with the infectious smile leaned down and gave me a hug, then he jumped down the steps taking all three at once. The beautiful girl with my heart in her hands gave me a crooked smile and playfully kicked my shoe. I returned the crooked smile and threw in a wink as I opened the screen door.

"Eight o'clock," I shouted over my shoulder as I closed the screen.

"Eight thirty and wear a skirt," she shouted back.

Chapter Three

I hardly slept at all Thursday night. I woke up Friday morning slightly hung over and completely exhausted. Ironically, I had never felt better in my life. I danced to the kitchen, fed my cat and drank three cups of coffee. I stood in my closet for half an hour looking at all my skirts and decided that none were worthy of my date with an angel. I promised myself that I would go shopping during my two-hour break between classes. My wardrobe debate made me unusually late for work. I breezed through a shower and threw on some jeans, which were not acceptable even on a Friday. I made it to my first class with only minutes to spare. I couldn't seem to concentrate on my lecture. I found myself grinning and making bad jokes about the Bard and his manipulation of the English language.

I made it through my first three classes and started to head to the mall. As I walked out of my office, my secretary reminded me of the department luncheon. I was the department head and there was no way I could miss it to go skirt shopping. I glanced down at my jeans and looked up at my secretary in sheer terror. She snickered and pointed me toward her desk. Apparently she had come straight to work from an all-night date. She had her date clothes thrown in a duffel bag underneath her desk. I pulled out a wrinkled skirt that, fortunately, matched my pale blue oxford. I looked up at her in terror again. She kicked off her heels and told me that I couldn't have her hose, so I had better be clean-shaven. I thought about it for a moment then breathed a sigh of relief.

I made it through the luncheon with no one commenting on my lack of proper hosiery. I gave a charming little speech, and to this day I have no clue what I actually said. Everyone left in good spirits, so I figured I must have been congenial. I got back to my office and kissed my secretary on the forehead. Seeing as how I wasn't out as gay, this probably seemed a bit odd. The skirt was kind of sexy and very comfortable. I wasn't going to have time to make it to the mall. I offered to buy the skirt for twenty bucks. She said she'd take fifty but the shoes weren't for sale. I knew how much her salary was and felt that fifty was probably appropriate.

My last class was over at four. That left me more than four hours to do all my paperwork, go to the gym, clean my house and get dressed. It was going to be tight as Friday paperwork usually took about two hours. For the first time since I received my doctorate, I blew off my paperwork. I knew that my compulsiveness about completion would make me nutty, but I had priorities that for once didn't involve my job. I lingered a bit longer than usual at the gym paying extra attention to my abs and chest. I stayed in the sauna longer than normal as well hoping to relax a bit. I was a nervous wreck to be quite honest. I hit the liquor store for three bottles of wine, tequila, beer and rum. I got home, ran a quick mop over the hardwoods and cleaned both bathrooms. I changed my sheets hating myself for being the optimist and possible slut.

It was seven thirty when I finally made it to the shower. I took my time though, scrubbing, shaving and panicking. Why was this woman making me freak? I dried my hair, put on my makeup and got dressed in record time. The doorbell rang just as I stepped into my heels.

"Hello, beautiful, nice skirt." She was radiant.

"Thanks, it's my secretary's." Why the hell did I have to say that?

"Alrighty then, are we ready or is she bringing you some shoes?"

"We're all set"—I was dying already—"she said I couldn't have the shoes."

She led me down the steps and opened the door of her silver Porsche Boxter. I was impressed but didn't show it. I was also relieved to know that she didn't want me as a "sugar mamma." Now I was really curious as to what someone so young and smart and beautiful would want from an old nerd like myself. Knowing there was only one way to find out, I climbed into the car and fastened my seatbelt preparing for a wild ride.

"So, where are we going tonight?" I asked fearing the worst.

"To the city of course, I want to keep you hostage in my car for an hour."

"Probably more like half an hour in this car." I giggled. I actually giggled.

"Actually, more like twenty minutes" the tires squealed as she pulled away.

She turned up the stereo and shot me an evil grin. I noticed what was playing—The Temptations. Motown. I melted.

"Where do you go to school?" I hated the fact that I asked. She was my students' age.

"I got my undergrad where you teach. I am fixin' to start law school in California." She turned down the music.

"How is someone your age already in law school?"

"How is someone your age the head of the English Department?"

"I see you've done your homework." I beamed.

"Thus the reason I am in law school already."

We made it downtown in no time at all. I had to unclench my fists as the valet opened the car door. She led me in to a very crowded, trendy little bar. Most of the patrons were upscale women in tight dresses and stiletto heels. There was a band, a dance floor and several service areas. We were shown to a table near the front marked RESERVED.

"I'm gonna powder my nose, will you order me a whiskey sour?"

She headed toward the back of the bar and I did as I was told. The waiter returned with great speed with her whiskey and my martini. I usually don't drink martinis but something about the bar made it seem mandatory. As soon as she returned from the restroom, the band started playing.

"Is it going to be too loud for you sitting this close" she shouted.

"Don't worry, I can take out my hearing aids."

We shouted back and forth over the music for several hours. The drinks flowed, as did the conversation. We shared stories of our childhood, families, jobs and ex-lovers. We laughed at the same time and were quiet at the same time. We made lingering eye contact and occasionally touched the other's hair, hands and face. Out of routine, I checked my watch when the waiter brought another round.

"Is it late for you, lady?" She looked worried.

"Not at all, force of habit."

"Good, because the night's just begun. Finish your drink. I want to take you to my second favorite place in the world."

I downed my drink and was surprised to feel a little dizzy as I stood. I was hoping her second favorite place served food. She stood, flipped her hair and turned toward the door. I just stood there in awe. She didn't even look back at me as she reached out her hand. I took her hand and felt my stomach jump. She tightened her grip and I felt safe. We walked hand in hand down the street to the Laine Bar inside the Laine Hotel. It was my second favorite place too. I grinned from ear to ear as she opened the door.

We found two stools at the bar and settled in. I ordered a beer and she ordered two burgers, two tequila shots and a beer. After I heard her request I was ready to drop to my knees and propose marriage. I decided to wait a few more hours so I could make sure we shared the same opinions on religion, children, abortion and the biggie—the cat versus dog dilemma. I was allergic to dogs but had already rationalized that if she was a dog lover, I could learn to deal with it. I tried to find a casual way to bring it up.

"I am sure my cat is freaking out, I'm rarely out this late," I said.

"Well, I hope he has a lot of food. It may be a while till you get home."

"What about you, any fuzzy faces in your entryway?"

"None that I know of, although my brother has been known to show up unannounced. If this is your subtle way of finding out if I am a cat lover then I guess I need to confess. I have never had a cat, but some of my best friends are cats. I am not a fan of dogs, they tend to be a little too high maintenance for my schedule."

I melted for the tenth time that night.

We ate our burgers in silence while the band played cheesy cover songs. She ordered two more tequila shots while I was in the bathroom.

"Are you trying to get me drunk, kid?"

"Yes, ma'am. I want to remove the proverbial bug from your arse."

"Well, not to sound like a nervous Nellie, but doesn't one of us have to drive the Boxter north tonight?"

"You think I'd let you drive that car? You must be drunk." She smirked.

"Well, I'm not sure I'll let you drive it either." I was slurring.

"Then it's a good thing I got a room here in the hotel."

I was already breathing heavy when we got into the elevator.

There was something so sexy about the way she pushed the elevator button with my hand in hers.

"So, do you take all your dates to The Laine?"

"Honestly, I've never done this before. But if it works out well tonight, I may make it a tradition. I didn't hear you saying no." She leaned toward me.

"I figured it was this or risk imprisonment. Either way there might be handcuffs."

"Oh my! The professor made a kinky reference!"

"Stop calling me the professor. It makes me feel old or like a character on Gilligan's Island."

"What would you like me to call you?" Her voice was deep and raspy.

"Everyone calls me Doc, but in about an hour I will accept 'Oh, baby or Oh, God'."

She turned her head sideways and I started to lean in. Before my lips met hers for the first time, the elevator doors opened. She shoved me backward toward the rooms. I walked backward the whole way to the room without breaking contact with her eyes. As soon as the door closed behind us she took both my hands in hers. She raised them above my head, pushed me against the wall and kissed me. I had fully expected our first kiss to be sweet and gentle and slow. This kiss was deep and fast and I couldn't get enough. My entire body felt charged. Parts of me that I forgot existed suddenly started dancing. Slow moans involuntarily rose from my throat. We stood there, my body pinned against the wall, and kissed for an eternity that felt like mere seconds.

"I'd like to show you my favorite place in the world now," she said between kisses.

"And I'd like to go there now," I whispered.

Chapter Four

The rest of the night had its awkward moments that I hate to admit. I was very self-conscious and she was pure perfection. I hadn't really been with a lot of women in the past few years. I pretty much assumed I was bad in bed because I hadn't had a lot of experience with lesbian sex since I was in college. I guess you could use that it's-like-riding-a-bicycle analogy. Yes, there are definite similarities but I don't think the analogy is totally true. She managed to guide me and I struggled along doing my darnedest. She seemed very satisfied and I have to confess that it was the best sexual experience of my life. I made the mistake of continually apologizing for my performance. She finally told me to shut up and confessed that it was the best sex she had ever had as well. We played for hours and finally drifted off to sleep in each other's arms.

When I woke up the next morning, she was snoring away. I

watched her for a few minutes and tried not to freak out about the fact that I felt love toward her already. I really didn't want to be the stereotypical lesbian who was out house hunting after the third date. I wanted to take things slowly. Okay, sex on the first date was hardly slow but she did justify it by saying she had been watching me for several months before we met. For some reason that seemed perfectly logical to me, although, if it were anyone else, I might have been creeped out by the stalking reference.

I managed to slip out of the bed without waking her. I didn't pay much attention to the room the night before—I was slightly distracted. In the morning light, I noticed that it was an amazing suite. I felt really bad that she had spent so much money on our date. I promised myself I would make it up to her somehow. When I went into the bathroom, I was astonished. Placed neatly on the counter were makeup, two toothbrushes and all the necessary toiletries. I don't know how I didn't notice this when I used the bathroom the night before. I couldn't help but to be a snoop. I went to the closet and opened the doors. Inside was an entire wardrobe—jeans, shoes, dresses, robes, the works. I stood there awed for a few minutes then went back to the bathroom. I took a quick shower and brushed my teeth with the newer looking toothbrush. I put on one of the robes and crawled back into bed. She didn't move a muscle. I really wanted her to wake up. I decided to turn on the TV and found some classic Seventies cartoons. She finally stirred.

"Good morning," I whispered and touched her hip.

"Hey you! Thank God, it wasn't just a dream."

"Well, maybe not for you, but it was a dream come true for me." I laughed. She inched her way toward me and nestled her head on my shoulder.

"That was a hell of a first date. How can we ever top that?" I asked.

She didn't respond, she just wrapped her entire body around mine. We lay in that position for another fifteen minutes while she snored away and I watched "Sigmond the Sea Monster." Finally, she opened her eyes and spoke.

"Hey, you took a shower. You're not gonna leave me are you?"

"No, I just wanted to make the most of the room while you slept."

She smiled and let out a cute, squeaky yawn.

"This is a nice room you got us. It's amazing what amenities they put in suites these days." I was trying to be subtle.

"Isn't it?" She smirked. "You could practically live here."

"You know, I've already slept with you and there are basic things I don't even know about you," I tried again.

"Well, what would you like to know?" She yawned again.

"Just the basics. Where were your born? What kind of pizza do you like? What's your last name? Do you have any hobbies?" I didn't want to come right out and ask yet.

She stroked my hair and stretched out her legs. "Okay. I was born here. I like pepperoni. My last name is Laine and I play a little tennis."

"Is that Laine as in the Laine Hotel?" I was shocked.

"You know, I never noticed that before. I guess it is," she grinned.

"That answers my next question of do you live here? But I thought you said in your e-mail that we had the same zip code." I was a bit annoyed.

"Yes, I own a house right off campus. I only stay here when I have to work at the firm. It's a long drive in weekday traffic." She sounded defensive.

I lay there staring at her. I don't know if I was expecting an explanation or an apology. She didn't say anything; she just stared back. Finally I spoke.

"Any other secrets I need to know about? Have you ever worked at a carnival or been arrested?"

"Nope. No more secrets. I own a hotel and am falling in love with an older woman."

I don't know which remark shocked me more. I pulled off my robe and rolled on top of her. She wrapped her legs around me and kissed my neck. Suddenly she stopped and spoke.

"Does that freak you out?"

"No, half the women I date own some sort of historic property."

"I mean the part about falling in love with an older woman," she asked.

"Yes, it really does freak me out."

"Really?"

"Yup, I don't think I am that much older than you."

My new friend hopped in the shower while I did a little channel surfing. I was tickled to discover that owning a hotel meant that you got all the porno movies for free twenty-four hours a day. That alone would be worth investing in a hotel. Suddenly I felt like Julia Roberts in "Pretty Woman" left alone in an incredible hotel suite. I was giddy. I wasn't so much excited that I met a rich woman, as I knew it would probably be awkward at times. I was excited that I had become smitten before I knew all the goodies about her. Just when I thought she couldn't get any better, I heard her singing in the shower. I crept to the bathroom door to listen more closely. She was doing some sort of Carol Channing impression. I heard the water cut off and dove back to the bed.

She exited the bathroom wearing a robe and had a towel turban on her head.

"Is that the great Carol Channing entering the room?" I teased.

"I guess I should be embarrassed but at least my impression was good enough to be deciphered." She pulled the towel off her wavy brown hair. "So, I assume that your calendar is clear for the next few days?"

"Well, today and tomorrow anyway." I was anxious to hear the agenda.

"As I recall, Monday is a holiday. Aren't you off?"

I scanned my memory. She was right. Usually I work on government holidays but decided to make an exception just this once.

"Well, today, tomorrow and Monday anyway." I was hyper.

"I took the liberty of coming up with some ideas." She opened her robe for a second and flashed me while she spoke. "I will list the options and you pick one or two."

"Okay, shoot."

"How would you like to sneak off to Vegas for a little roulette and Wayne Newton?"

I was uncomfortable with this—I didn't have the money it took to dash off on a whim. I wasn't about to take advantage of her fortune although I was sure she would be okay with it. It sounded wonderful though. I loved spontanaiety.

"Wow, that's a really great offer for a girl like me." I hoped she caught the reference.

"Okay, Vivian." She did. "Or we could find out what's going on in the ballroom downstairs and crash the party."

"Why do I get the feeling that you crash a lot of parties?"

"Hey, a gal's gotta eat, right?" She flashed me again.

I adored her confidence and the fact that she enjoyed teasing me.

"What else ya got?" I was sure she was filled with great ideas.

"Actually, that's all I came up with. I figured you would go for the Vegas thing."

"Well, to be honest, unless you own a casino and an airline, I really can't afford last minute travel." I wanted to crawl into a hole.

"As a matter of fact—" She was smirking. "Don't worry, I'm kidding. My properties are hardly mafia related. Don't worry about the funding. I will grab the tab this weekend and you can get it next time."

"Oh, already assuming there will be a next time?"

"I'm confident there will be," she said as she towel-dried her hair.

"I would feel better if we got to know each other a bit first before I started taking advantage of my new sugar mama. Tell me more about this party-crashing addiction of yours."

"It's a lot of fun. I find out what the occasion is, buy a gift so I'm not empty-handed and dress appropriately. I've been to tons of wedding receptions, anniversary parties, birthdays, bar mitzvahs and even a prom."

"What's the occasion today?"

"I think it's an evening wedding reception, but I can make sure."

"What do you do if it's a sit-down formal dinner?"

"I tell the kitchen to add two more places and don't charge the guest."

"So is this another thing you do with all your dates?" I didn't want to be ordinary.

"No, usually I go with my brother. I did take a date to the prom though."

I was afraid to ask. "Was this a boy date or did you crash the prom with a woman?"

"It was a boy. I didn't need the press hearing from all the freaked-out teenagers."

"So, are you bi?" I never thought to ask and prayed she wasn't.

"No, ma'am. But I am not out to the public, just to family. I put on a straight face when necessary. I usually dress up a gay boy if I know dancing will be mandatory."

I wasn't sure I was comfortable with having to help her hide but understood the reasons.

"Are you sure you want to be seen at a reception with me?"

"Positive. We just need to show some discretion." She flashed me again.

"Yes, you seem very discreet."

She threw off the robe completely and came running toward the bed. I pulled the covers up over my head and balled up in the fetal position. She tugged at the belt on my robe and I didn't budge. She sang my name and I still didn't uncurl. Finally she tickled me and I had to move for fear of the worst. I quickly flipped over and straddled her. Right as she started to lower my robe, room service knocked on the door.

"Argh!" I whispered.

"Run, Forrest, run!" She giggled, got up and put on her robe.

I hurried out from under the covers and hid in the bathroom. I heard her in the next room carrying on a lengthy conversation like she and the room service guy were old friends. I sat down on the bathtub ledge and knocked a shampoo bottle into the tub. It struck me as funny, then I realized how annoyed she might be if I outed her in front of one of her employees. I sat there frozen for several minutes longer. Finally I heard the door close but I didn't dare move. I no longer heard any voices but remained still, assuming she would get me when the coast was clear. I sat there in silence for ten minutes and decided to test the waters. I cracked open the bathroom door and glanced toward the bedroom. She was seated at the table eating a croissant. I tiptoed to the room.

"Is he gone?"

"Yup." She stared at the TV.

"Why didn't you come get me?"

"Well, you were so quiet, I forgot you were here." She smiled.

"I am so sorry, I hope he didn't interrogate you." I felt awful.

"He didn't care. He is the gay boy I took to prom."

"Then why did you leave me in there?"

"I don't know. I just really like fucking with you." She grinned like a cat eating chicken.

"What have I gotten myself into?" I blushed when she said the f-word.

"I will assume that is a rhetorical question. Have some breakfast. I didn't know what you liked, so I took the liberty of ordering everything on the menu."

"If I forget to tell you later, I had a really good time tonight."

"You're good." She threw a bagel at me.

Chapter Five

Three Years Later

We had lived together less than a week and it was finally Friday night, finally our first weekend together. Saturday was upon us, the first morning we could sleep in together and be lazy all day if we wanted. The whole week was pretty much chaos. I picked her up at the airport Sunday afternoon and we spent half the night retrieving her necessities from the storage unit. Monday through Friday we hardly saw each other. I had to get up at five in the morning to fight traffic and be at work at eight. She started her new job immediately upon arrival, going in at nine and getting home late, hours after the office closed. We were both so exhausted this first week that we just unpacked boxes at night, ate and fell asleep during the late news. It was not what I expected after waiting over three years to share a home, but it was understandable with all the changes and work at hand.

But Friday night had arrived and I was exhilarated at the thought of getting to see her all weekend. I got home at about seven and started cooking dinner. She called at nine and said she'd be home late because some clients insisted on taking her to dinner. I was disappointed for me but happy for her. She had landed her dream job and to already have such good clients was a big deal. I fought sleep until about eleven and eventually drifted off. She tiptoed in around midnight, pulled off her clothes, crawled into bed and was asleep within minutes.

I still wasn't totally used to sharing a bed with her. For the most part, I had slept alone for quite some time. Around four a.m. I felt my pillow being stripped away from me. I rolled over to steal it back, but instead, just laid my head beside hers, our faces inches from each other. I could feel her breathing so peaceful and sweet. I moved my hand to her hip, she took a deep breath and sighed. Then she slowly opened her eyes and smiled at me. With no words spoken, she pulled herself closer and went back to sleep with her lips pressed up against my neck. A few minutes later she started kissing my neck and worked her way around to my lips. Suddenly we were kissing passionately, the first passionate kisses we had shared since her last visit.

I carefully moved myself on top of her and she wrapped her entire body around mine. Our breathing grew heavier and still no words were spoken. I had waited for this moment all week and part of me wanted to go wild. But there was something so sweet about the way we found each other in the darkness that made me decide to be gentle and make gentle love to this beautiful woman. We stopped kissing and stared in each other's eyes. The light coming through the curtains was just enough that I could see every feature of my incredible partner. Her eyes were dancing, her lips were slightly apart, her chest was heaving and her delicate body was bathed in moonlight.

I went back in for a strong kiss that felt like it went on for hours. I slowly made my way down her body, kissing every soft inch, licking all the tender spots. When I arrived at her stomach (my favorite place), she timidly spread her legs apart, inviting me to go further. I slid my tongue down one thigh then up the other. She let out a growl and I melted. With desperate anticipation, I moved my tongue to her soft, trim V. She was soaked, so wet, in fact, that she was dripping. Feeling this against my tongue made me pour. I thought I was going to burst.

My tongue danced around the outside for a while, licking and teasing while I tenderly placed my finger inside her. I had fantasized about this all week long and doing it was a million times better. She let out a little stuttered moan, she was breathing so hard, and she whispered my name. I pulled my finger out, spread her apart and put my tongue inside her as deeply as I could. She tasted so sweet. Her taste was nearly indescribable—pure passion and excitement. I continued darting my tongue in and out, alternating it with my fingers and playing with her V with my other hand. Her body was flailing. She kept pushing my hand away, and then pulling it back. She was practically screaming and I flowed like a river. I wanted to kiss her so bad, but I didn't want to stop the licking. I wanted to feel her inside me, I wanted her to taste me but I just couldn't stop. I brought her to orgasm four times, stopping only long enough to catch my breath.

I moved my way back up her body, again kissing every inch. When I reached her lips, I could tell how tired she was—her eyes were fighting to stay open and her breathing was calm. I said, "Good night, sweet angel," and didn't expect a reply. I rolled to my side and tried to go to sleep. A minute later, she rolled over and spooned me, whispering in my ear, "It's good to be home." We both drifted to sleep.

When I awoke Saturday morning, our room was unusually bright. I panicked thinking that I had overslept until mid-afternoon and missed the day I had waited so long for. The clock said eight-seventeen. The room was bright because my darling girl had opened the mini-blinds that overlooked the back deck. I knew what this meant. I walked to the window to confirm my suspicion. Yep, she was out there floating on the pool, in my swimsuit! Already she was stealing my wardrobe! I went to the kitchen. The coffee was made and the cat was fed, which was nice since she hated my sweet cat. Stuck to a box of warm doughnuts was a note—I STOLE YOUR SUIT, MINE'S IN A BOX SOMEWHERE, GUESS YOU'LL HAVE TO WEAR YOUR OLD BIKINI . . . BUMMER.

It was so weird to have things already done when I woke up. We bought this house together four months ago and since then, I have lived alone while she finished grad school out of state. All week long I had been up hours before her, so the coffee and food were a rare treat. I was tempted to skip the doughnuts, knowing I was fixin' to wedge myself into a bikini but she did take the time to go get them and I noticed she had already eaten four. That's my girl. I grabbed two, a cup of coffee and the TV remote (out of habit). Taped to the remote was a note—WHAT COULD POSSIBLY BE ON THAT'S MORE EXCITING THAN WHAT'S WAITING OUTSIDE? Good point. I scarfed my food and danced to the bedroom. Then I did what all women do when they put on swimwear—shave, tuck, look, complain. Oh well. I figured she couldn't run now, her name was on the mortgage too.

I grabbed a towel and headed outside. She had been busy. The CD changer was playing. The cooler was iced down with beer, wine, water, hamburger patties—all the makings of a day outdoors. I guess she figured the unpacking could wait too. As I approached the pool, she didn't even look my way, then I realized she was asleep. I couldn't resist, I had to cannonball. I walked back about ten feet, turned around and started a slow jog toward the deep end. On the last step, I tripped on a boulder (okay, a pebble) and slipped face first into the water. When I came up, my top was floating beside me and she was laughing her ass off. I couldn't help but blush.

"I thought you were asleep."

"I was but I woke up when I heard the pitter-patter of huge feet."

"So you saw the whole incident?"

"Just the good parts and I'm glad to see you already took your top off, saves me the trouble."

"Funny, throw it here before the neighbors call the cops."

"The cops? You mean they'd send women in uniform over here to handcuff you?"

She was such a nut. I splashed water and dove under to put my top back on.

I didn't know what to do next. I really wanted to take her inside and jump her in the shower. But she obviously had a day planned, so I didn't want to ruin her homecoming. I swam up to the neon lounger and grabbed her feet. She playfully kicked and shot me the biggest grin. I dove underwater and started swimming the length of the pool. I had been doing laps every day, and thought that today was no different—boy was I wrong. On my way back to the shallow end, she met me halfway, tackling me in a sort of crocodile roll. I wrapped myself around her and pulled her to the surface. When both our heads were above water, she leaned in like she was going to kiss me, then she placed her hands on my shoulders and shoved me under water. Afterward, she swam away and climbed back up on her perch. I gathered my composure, not wanting to admit that I had just inhaled a gallon of water, and swam toward the stairs. As I paddled past her, she ran her hand along the length of my body. Damn, I wanted to climb on that air mattress with her and rock the boat. Instead I got out of the pool and dried myself off.

"Where are you going?"

"To get some more coffee and some sunscreen. Oh, and I'm going to grab some CDs—the ones you put in are too heavy for this early."

"Yes, I forgot your no-guitar-solos-before-ten-a.m. rule."

I poured the coffee into a thermos and rummaged through her boxes of music. I was so impressed that she had packed them alphabetically. By the time I was at the Cowboy Junkies (C, not J), I felt her arms wrap around my stomach. She placed her chin on my shoulder and said, "Sheryl Crowe." I grabbed it and set it aside. Then she said "Please, no Damn Yankees," while she started kissing my neck. I reached behind me and put my hands on the back of her thighs. She pulled her hands from my waist and unhooked my top while kissing my shoulders. I made a clumsy attempt to turn my body around and she stopped me.

"I just want to kiss you."

"Then you shouldn't look so good in that swimsuit."

"I look better in the one piece."

"Not better than I look in it."

"True, you look like a goddess."

She really did, her light hair fell to her shoulders and framed her face like a work of art.

"Well, if you just want kisses then turn around. Otherwise quit talking so much and lay your back against my chest."

I was surprised by her aggressiveness but I didn't argue.

I was still seated Indian-style and she moved off her knees and placed her legs on either side of me. I leaned my dry back against her wet swimsuit as ordered. She continued kissing my neck and shoulders and began caressing my breasts. I wanted to kiss her so desperately! The way she gently stroked my stomach made me feel so safe. She lowered her hands to my wet bikini bottoms and I adjusted myself so I could pull them off.

"Keep them on," she whispered, "I just want to tease you for a while, we have all day." She wrapped one arm around my waist and put her other hand on my crotch. I surprised myself by letting out a quick moan. It seemed like it had been forever since she touched me—it was a month from the time when she last visited. She started moving her hand in tender circular motions. Then she gradually pressed harder and increased speed.

I wanted her inside me. I didn't want a quick playtime but she seemed to have the day planned and I didn't want to argue. My hips started dancing, my breathing got stronger and I started moaning.

"Are you close?" She whispered.

"Yes," I squeaked as quietly as I could.

She pressed her body taut against mine and squeezed me tighter and next she said, "Do you want to finish or do you want to kiss?"

I can't believe I said this, but I adore this woman's kisses. "I want to kiss you." She didn't seem surprised and she didn't miss a beat. She stopped the circles, crawled around me and straddled my lap. The second her lips touched mine I reached orgasm. This was an amazing woman. She gave me a choice and I got both. We sat in that same position and kissed for another half hour. We only stopped because my legs fell asleep.

Chapter Six

My mind-blowing companion grabbed a doughnut and headed back to the pool. I proceeded to gather CDs and regain my composure. I was a little shocked and severely swept away by her latest attack. I took my time before joining her in the backyard—I didn't want my age to show by looking too flustered and amazed. She was putting more ice in the cooler and spilled a good portion of it on the deck. I just stood there and watched her bend over to pick up the little pieces and add them to the cooler. She was adorable, no, unbelievable, with perfect cleavage when she reached down. I wanted to see the backside view, so I informed her that she dropped some ice behind her. She shot me a grin and a wink, knowing what I was up to, then turned around and bent over. I couldn't help myself—I burst out laughing. I choked so hard that coffee rolled up my throat and out my nose. Her swimsuit was wedgie-fied in her butt. I was caught off guard by the depth of this wedgie, thinking it might take a set of tongs and a surgeon to remove it.

"Going for the polyester enema this morning?" I asked through giggles.

"You like that? I wanted make sure my ass got your attention."

"Lady, your ass could get my attention hidden under a pile of poodles."

"Yes, but it wouldn't make you laugh as much."

"True, I'm not a huge fan of poodles."

She finished her icing duties and dove into the pool. I got distracted with a cluster of weeds along the fence. I knew I couldn't enjoy myself knowing there was a pile of dandelions staring me in the eye all day. The problem with weeds is once you start pulling one group, you inevitably find another group. The next thing I knew, I had a huge mound of dead weeds next to me and some of them were blowing into the pool.

"Hey, Mr. Greenjeans, you gonna do that all day? You're turning the pool into a mudslide and you haven't looked up in twenty minutes. Am I boring you?"

"No, time flies, sorry. I'm not used to having you here, I'm easily preoccupied."

"Well, get in the pool, it's too hot for yard work."

I put the weeds in the compost pile, swept up the dirt and started a slow jog toward the deep end. Halfway there, I remembered my earlier slip and walked the rest of the way. Instead of diving or cannonballing, I sat on the edge and lowered myself into the water. I doggie paddled toward my new live-in as she patted the water and shouted "Here, girl!" When I got close enough, she stroked my hair, "Good, girl!" she said. I panted.

"Hey, you're getting burned, did you get the sunscreen?"

"Yeah, it's by the stereo, I'll get it." I said as I climbed out of the pool.

"Dry off and I'll put some on your back." She said as she followed me out.

I adored the idea of having a beautiful girl rub oil on my back. I laid facedown on the chaise lounge, handed her the SPF 25 and she straddled me. I let out my usual little growl and blushed. She squirted the lotion on my shoulders and spread it out in circular motions. She concentrated on my shoulders for a few minutes, turning the simple task into an elaborate massage. Then she unhooked my top and worked her way down my back. She "accidentally" slipped down the sides and under a few times, which really got my attention. Then I felt her stand, which I took as encouragement to roll over so she could do my front. I couldn't have been more wrong. She was getting up because the old lady from next door was watching us over the fence. Unfortunately, I didn't realize this until I was completely topless and lying on my back. My masseuse threw a towel at me and spoke to the neighbor.

"Hey, there! How are you today?"

"I'm fine. I see you two are having a nice day as well."

"Oh, hello, Mrs. Jacobs. How's the garden?" I chimed in awkwardly.

"It's being eaten by rabbits or bugs. I'm trying to put up some wire."

"I'm sorry to hear that. You haven't met my partn—"

"You don't have to introduce me, I know all about her." The old lady interrupted.

I wasn't sure how to take that. I panicked thinking maybe the homeowners association had a meeting about what to do with the token dykes. Then I remembered I had told Mrs. Jacobs all about our relationship at the neighborhood garage sale. She was cool about it and even shared a story of a hotsie totsie she knew in the Sixties.

"Well, I won't keep you girls, you seem to be full of activity. I just wanted to steal some more of your compost, if that's okay." She shouted over the music.

"Sure, take all you want, do you want me to bring it over? I can do it right now." I shouted back, not so much because of the music, it wasn't loud—she was deaf.

"No, no hurry, keep your shirt on." She quipped and laughed hysterically.

Then she disappeared below the fence. My mate and I made eye contact and burst into wild chuckles. "I'm gonna like it here," she shouted, hoping the lady would hear. Still laughing, I fired up the coals for the barbecue. Neither one of us said much while we ate. We just stared at each other, giggled and blushed.

We were both a little sleepy after the heat, beer, food and embarrassment. We elected to head inside to drift off rather than risk massive sunburn and possible drowning. It was good timing, as some ominous clouds were moving into the area. We gathered our things, tied down the air mattresses and turned off the music, It was after noon, so she was back to the monster ballads.

"You want to shower and watch a movie?" I asked, hoping for the shower time.

"Nah, let's wait and shower before we go out tonight. A movie's good though."

"Are we going out tonight? I thought we'd stay in and cook."

"You promised to show me the town on my first free night, I fully intend on seeing the places you've been frequenting for four months." She insisted.

"Okay, think about what mood you're in—dinner, dancing, music, tattoos, piercings, strip clubs, freak shows, festivals, roller coasters, you name it."

"Wow, you get around! I was thinking we could go see a band somewhere."

"Okay, I know a few places, in fact there's one within walking distance." I'd been there too many lonely nights in four months, but it was safe for drinking and not driving.

We both changed out of our suits into boxers and tees. There was little flirtation, we were both burned and exhausted. I followed her into the den and closed the blinds while she picked a DVD.

We had accumulated quite a collection during our many visits of staying in and ordering pizza. I pretty much knew what she'd pick—some sort of soppy chick flick. I was surprised to see her put "The Breakfast Club" into the DVD player. Now came the crucial decision—where to sit. Our den was furnished with a sofa, love seat, recliner, ottoman and hard wooden chair. I knew if she chose anything but the sofa, I had to sit alone. She made a beeline to the sofa. I stood there looking lost until she motioned me to join her. I danced to her side and plopped down like a good little puppy. She quickly positioned herself, lying on her back with her head propped on some pillows. I nestled myself between her legs and laid my head on her thigh. This was our usual movie-watching position. I don't know why I hesitated.

She pressed play on the remote and stroked my damp hair. I was torn between the comfort of sleep and the excitement of my position. I made it through the drop-off-at-detention scene of the movie and started to drop off myself. I noticed the hair-stroking had stopped and looked up to see my cutie sleeping hard with her mouth open. I decided to let myself nap, but my mind raced. In my head I was trying to plan the perfect evening—what to wear, what time to go, things to talk about, etc. I even had a scenario in my mind about how the night would end.

Before I knew it, the movie was nearly over and I slept little. I heard her yawn then felt her scratching my back. I nestled my head in harder against her thigh. Her body stirred and readjusted. The scratching stopped and I heard her breathing hard. I assumed she went back to sleep, so I attempted to do the same. Suddenly her hips moved slightly and she started breathing even harder. I realized that she was not asleep but just as aroused as I was. I rolled off my side, on to my stomach, placing my face, well, basically in her crotch. I put my hands on her hips and started moving them up and down, slowly. She lifted her hips, pushing herself against my mouth. I nibbled a little on the outside of her boxers and reached for the waistband. She lifted herself up and helped me pull the cotton off her body. While I pulled the shorts down and over her feet, she took off her shirt and tugged at mine. I finished undressing her and removed my clothing in two quick motions.

I climbed up her beautiful body and spread my legs on either side of her. With our breasts pressed together, I leaned in for a long, hard kiss. I felt my face get hot and the river pour. She wrapped her arms around me so tightly that I felt like I was breathing for the both of us. I leaned back, pressing our trimmed areas against each other. I rocked back and forth for a few minutes, making us both wetter and wetter. Then, I moved my right leg, placing my whole body to the side of her and dragged my hand between her cleavage, over her tummy and down her thigh. I moved my fingers back up her other thigh and slowly entered her. She looked deeply into my eyes and sensually bit her bottom lip. I pushed my finger deeper inside her, pulled it out then went back in with two fingers. Her hips started swaying and soft moans rose from her throat.

Outside the thunder roared, lightning struck and the rain pounded against the widows. Inside I felt safe and sound, inside the house and inside my lover. Finally, after four months, I felt secure in my environment like nothing could hurt me. I felt peaceful, I felt love, I felt security. My princess moaned with the thunder, shook with the lightning and pounded with the rain. When she finished, I crawled on top of her and found comfort in her arms. I huddled my face in her neck. I found solace in her body. I simply collapsed on top of her and never felt so relaxed in my life. We held each other long past the end of the movie, past the end of the storm and into the early hours of evening.

Eventually we had to move. I always felt like I was crushing her if I stayed for more than five minutes. I lost forty-five pounds and still felt like a big girl. She claimed to be tough but I still saw her as a delicate flower. The image of an elephant on top of a mouse made me finally get up. She argued, claiming that the human blanket was keeping her warm. I debated, stating that the human blanket was cutting off airflow to her lungs. I won mainly because she had to answer the phone. We had smart ring—one ring was for me, two rings were for her. It was her work. I was annoyed thinking they were calling her in. I eavesdropped: "Uh-huh, okay, right, okay, I will . . . yes, see you Monday." I was relieved and pretended I didn't care. She didn't explain after she hung up the phone. She merely stood up, walked over to me and gave me the biggest hug imaginable. I didn't want to let go, neither did she. I think it was the longest hug I've ever had.

We paused in the kitchen long enough to grab a bottle of champagne and some crystal flutes then proceeded to the bedroom. I followed her in and we both sat on the edge of the bed as she poured the Moët into the glasses.

"Here's to our first Saturday." She lifted her glass.

"Here's to every Saturday, forever." I toasted.

We clinked, kissed, drank and at the same time, threw our glasses into the fireplace. I was amazed that I actually did it and even more shocked that she had the same idea. I know it was driving us both nuts to have broken glass in the bedroom fireplace, but neither of us gave it a second thought. In fact, we both giggled and passed the bottle back and forth. We sat there for twenty minutes making silly toasts—here's to broken glass . . . here's to bloody feet . . . here's to expensive crystal . . . here's to shopping for more crystal. Finally the bottle was empty and we were laughing so hard that the toasts made no sense. I think the last one was here's to Mrs. Jacobs and her pile-o-compost.

"Do you want to shower first?" I asked in a buzzed slur.

"Well, part of the reason we bought the house was for the dual showerheads, so I think we can go together, that is if you don't mind," she slurred back.

"Well, I guess that's okay but I'm kinda shy, you know."

"I know you're shy. You only hesitated three minutes while the neighbor checked out your rack," she retorted.

"Hey, sometimes you gotta give an old lady a thrill."

"I know, that's why I flirt with you as much as possible."

"Careful . . . I have a weak heart. And I'm only six years older, not sixty."

She rose from the bed, pulled off her clothes and started the showers. I set the champagne bottle by the door then felt nutty and threw it into the fireplace. At the same time, I made a wish—*let this moment last forever*. Then I pulled my clothes off and followed her into the shower. We stood on opposite ends under our individual showerheads and washed our hair. While we watched each other soap up and shave, I had the craziest thought. I wondered what would happen if I finished my shower and just walked out. I hurried through the lather, the conditioner and the rinse. I turned off my half of the shower, squeegeed the glass and walked toward the door. As I started to step out, she grabbed me around the neck. I was afraid my 31-year-old body scared her off. I immediately turned around, placed my hands on her hips and pulled her close. We kissed in the steam until the hot water was gone. When we were done, we left the glass un-squeegeed, which drove me nuts, but we were together so I didn't mind. We dried each other and in a drunken stupor, decided to pick out each other's clothes.

My confidante still hadn't unpacked her casual clothes, so we only had my wardrobe to choose from. This was a daunting task as most of my clothes were either ten years old or very conservative. She was more of a laid back, sexy type of dresser. She dressed me in tight jeans, a black oxford with three buttons undone and black Nocona's. For her I chose khaki hip huggers, a white stretch shirt with three buttons undone and suede mules. Neither of us was happy with how we looked but we were both delighted with the other. We finished our makeup individually and headed toward the door.

Chapter Seven

Part of the appeal of our house was its location. We resided in a sort of arts district, close to galleries, bars, restaurants and antique stores. It was a diverse neighborhood and residents spanned the spectrum from the eccentric old people to the young yuppie couples. I considered us to be eccentric yuppies with a twist. I just assumed with the vast number of laid-back artists around, our lifestyle would be no big deal. I walked down to the bars alone many times but never thought to look for other gay couples. As my partner and I crossed the street hand-in-hand, I felt a bit awkward. She didn't seem to have any problem—it never bothered her when people stared at us. I, on the other hand, had a hard time feeling comfortable. I still had difficulty accepting the fact that I was different. We didn't look different, neither of us was butch, in fact we were both feminine and usually had to put up with men hanging on us in bars. She made me promise that when we moved in together, I would drop my inhibitions and be proud of what a beautiful couple we made. Tonight I made it a priority to be less reticent.

We arrived at The Attic, a trendy spot packed with young, mod people. The doorman was delighted to welcome us and our twenty-dollar cover. We made our way through the crowds and settled at the corner of the bar. There was only one stool, so I insisted that she sit, knowing that I'd probably have to get up more with my small bladder. I stood beside her and leaned against the bar. She finally managed to get someone's attention after waving her arms in the air for five minutes—such a subtle and demure lady. When the bartender headed to our end, I felt my face get red and I knew what was about to happen. I panicked and dropped my date's hand.

"Well, hey Professor!" The bartender shouted and reached her hand out to me.

"Hey yourself! It's Emily, right?" I shook her hand ineptly.

"No, it's Emma. I'm in your Monday, eight o'clock." She blushed.

"Right, third row. I hope you got your paper done already."

"Of course, you gave us three weeks. You're very generous with your assignments. Most teachers only give us a few days. What can I get y'all?"

"I'll have a rum and diet and she will have a Tom Collins."

"No, SHE will have a screwdriver, thank you," my mate stated, annoyed.

Emma disappeared and returned with two very strong drinks. She set mine in front of me and then whispered to my angry companion before setting the glass on a coaster.

"What do I owe you, Emma?"

"It's on me, Professor. Just remember that when you check my grammar."

"You are very generous as well. I will remember that."

I felt a cold stare and knew what was coming. I must have

looked like a deer caught in the headlights when I turned around because my demure pal exploded into laughter. I was totally confused. She finds my embarrassment and panic amusing?

"Got a little nervous there, eh? Afraid the hot professor might get outed?"

"I'm sorry. I just never expected to see my students. I never really thought about it. We are sixty miles from campus." I spoke quickly.

"Is that why we moved out here? So you could hide?"

"No, we moved out here for the culture, the incredible, historic house and so you could be close to work," I confidently retorted.

"Aren't you dying to know what Emma said to me?"

"I was afraid to ask. I thought she might tell you what a dork I am."

"I already know what a dork you are. She told me she just won the class pool."

"Please tell me you're joking. Tell me my sexuality was not discussed in class."

"Yup. You have just entered the spank bank of every gay coed in English one-o-one."

I pretty much wanted to crawl into a hole at that point. I was already dreading going to work Monday morning. I wanted to slam my drink and run home screaming. I looked around the bar avoiding eye contact with every woman I saw. I looked down at my boots and kicked the barstool. My sweet love took my hand and kissed it. I felt better. I smiled.

"Hey Emma! What was the pool up to?" I shouted over the band.

"A hundred and seventy-five and a free hour of bowling." She laughed.

"Well, then, it looks like you owe me a few more drinks."

"Coming right up, Doctor. Anything for family."

We stayed at The Attic for one more drink and decided to leave because the band sucked. My apologies to The Windows but if

Jim Morrison wasn't dead before, he is now. We made our way to the street and saw a line of tone-deaf people waiting to go in. I desperately wanted a bullhorn so I could warn them all: *Aside from the cute bartender, there is nothing to see here. Please go back to your homes and in the future avoid all tribute bands.* Alas, I had no bullhorn, so we just strolled across the street to the next bar. We handed the bouncer our IDs and he asked us for ten bucks. I reached into my pocket to get the cash when the genius beauty stopped me.

"Let's just go home. I can think of better things to do than sit in crowds."

"You don't want to wait an hour for a drink and listen to bad bands?" I asked.

"No, we can come back Monday or Wednesday when it's calmer, let's go."

This was true. I didn't really have to be on campus until ten on Tuesdays and Thursdays. I was a little worried though, she seemed upset and her suggestion to leave was abrupt and surprising considering how much she wanted to go out. It was still early, this was so unlike her. We walked back across the street and headed toward home. I picked up the pace a bit as the rain started pouring. She grabbed the back of my shirt and stopped me. She just stood there in the middle of the storm and stared at me.

"Are you okay, do you feel all right?" I worried.

"I'm fine. I just wanted to look at you."

"I look like a drowned rat. You look like one too." I started to walk.

She pulled the back of my shirt again. I stopped and looked in her eyes. It was hard to tell from the rain, but I think she was crying. I reached for her hand. She pulled it away. I panicked—she never turned away from my touch before. Just as I started to speak, she placed both hands on my face and kissed me. My heart raced and my stomach relaxed. We stood there in the middle of the street, kissing and getting soaked. Suddenly a huge crash of thunder hit, and we both made a mad dash to the house.

She unlocked the door and took off her shoes. She was so cute, dripping wet, balancing herself on the coat rack, trying to pull wet shoes off wet feet. I couldn't help myself. The minute she pulled off the second shoe, I attacked her. I pushed the coat rack out of the way and shoved her against the wall. I pressed my stomach hard against hers and she put her arms on my shoulders. She wrapped her left leg around my waist, and followed with her right as she tightened her arms around my shoulders. I instinctively placed my arms down to support her as her back flattened against the wall. Her chest was heaving. I could feel her heart pounding. Maybe it was my heart I could feel, maybe they were in unison.

She lowered her arms and I leaned my upper body back as she started to unbutton my shirt. I was chilled as the air hit my chest and the rainwater rolled into my cleavage. She fumbled with her own buttons, pulled her shirt back and pushed her damp bra up above her voluptuous breasts. I immediate moved toward her right side with my lips, kissing the breast hard then teasing the nipple with my tongue. She liberated a soft moan as she pushed the wet hair out of my face. I moved my attention to her left side then settled my face between the two while I caught my breath. The hardwood floor under us was slippery from the pool of water that dripped from our bodies. I adjusted my position and carried her down the steps into the living room. I slowly and ungracefully lowered us to the carpet. She untucked my shirt and finished opening the last few buttons. I pulled it off in six clumsy motions.

The beauty tugged on my belt as I fumbled with my bra. I removed the belt for her in one fast whipping sound. She pulled her shirt and bra completely off and moved the wet hair out of her eyes. We unbuttoned each other's pants and feverishly kissed. We rolled around on the rough carpet for an hour—damp, cold and euphoric. We were home.

Chapter Eight

We tiptoed to the bedroom in darkness. The power went out somewhere between her second orgasm and my third. I fumbled for some candles on the dresser while she retrieved robes and towels from the bathroom. She handed me a robe and took the towels to the entryway. I watched in candlelight as she fought with the cat to soak up the water off the floor. He wanted to play but she was not amused. She pushed the towel across the floor and the cat chased it while attaching his claws to the end. She pulled it away fast which only made him more playful. Finally she gave in and danced the towel along the perimeter of the hall while he chased it. After a few minutes of cat and mouse, she threw the wet towel over his body and walked off. He stared at her dejected, looked at me and licked his paws. I think he might have decided to keep her. I know I did.

We made our way to the kitchen and settled in at the barstools.

The radio was dead, no batteries. I don't know why the thought of sitting in silence made me nervous—perhaps it was her odd behavior on the street. I pulled an old transistor from the drawer. No batteries.

"Take the ones from the remote."

"Wrong size, but smart thinking, what would I do without you?"

"You'd probably watch a lot of porn and drink too much." She replied.

The sad thing is, I really did drink and watch porn a lot while she was off at school. I would never admit it though. I would never confess to being an alcoholic pervert.

"So what happened on the street? You had me worried for a minute."

"I don't know. I think I suddenly realized that today is the beginning of a whole new life. It struck me that I was spending it with you. I freaked for a minute."

"That's comforting that the thought of living with me freaks you out." I pronounced.

"On the contrary. We waited so long for this to finally happen. I was really scared that it wouldn't work. But sitting there with you tonight, surrounded by strangers, I felt safe. When I stopped you on the street and looked in your eyes, I saw something I've never seen before. I saw myself through your eyes. You kinda like me." She smiled.

"Kinda. The cat really likes you though. I guess you can stay."

She just rolled her eyes and bit her lip. I'm sure there was a euphemism in there somewhere, but neither of us wanted to spoil the moment.

"So, what's the plan for tomorrow?" she asked.

"Well, after church, I usually play bingo or bridge."

"Right, then you volunteer at the Republican headquarters."

"Of course. You know me too well." I laughed. "I figured we really need to get you unpacked and we need to think about furnishing this empty house. It echoes."

"We have furniture in the den, we have a bed and two barstools, what's left?"

"Um, the office, three guest rooms, a living room, a dining room—"

"Okay, I got it, we have to act like normal adults."

"Well, we can try. Just in case we ever have company."

I was a little worried about buying furniture with her. We had very different tastes but we made a deal to do it together so we will both feel at home. I've lived in an empty house all this time, it would be weird to actually have a place to do my paperwork other than the kitchen floor.

"What do you want to do now? Eat? Swim? Sleep? Shower?" I offered.

"So many choices. Would it be okay if I said I just wanted to go to bed?"

"Of course that's okay, we've had an . . . um . . . exhausting day."

"Gonna join me?" She smiled.

"I'll be in soon. I have to reset the clocks and check for leaky windows."

"I'll save you a warm spot."

"You are my warm spot."

Chapter Nine

We stayed up much later than expected. I will not give details—at this point what happened was a given. I will say that I was happy the neighbor was hard of hearing. I slept until eight and when I awoke, my bunkmate was snoring away in my ear. She claimed that she never snored. I will say that I wish I were hard of hearing. I managed to slide out of bed without waking her and made my way to the shower. I did my best to be quiet, but it is impossible for me to shower without singing, especially after the Saturday I had. So, I lathered, rinsed and repeated while singing (as quietly as possible) "The Happening" by the Supremes. Yes, an odd shower song for a woman my age, but a happy song nonetheless. I finished my morning routine, glanced in to see if she was still sacked out—she was, so I skulked to the kitchen.

Kitty and I settled down to coffee and crosswords. I thought about making breakfast but I wasn't sure if she ate breakfast and I never thought to ask. During most of our visits, we traveled and usually ordered coffee from room service. It's funny how I didn't know such an important detail about someone I lived with. I sat there thinking about all the other things about her I didn't know and might want to find out. I wondered how often she called her family. I wondered what she bought at the grocery store, what brands she chose, what flavors of Pop-Tarts, what kind of cookies. I hoped it was blueberry and Oreos. I wondered if she peed in the shower and if she read on the toilet. I decided to find out the grocery and family stuff. I really didn't want to know the bathroom behavior.

Suddenly from the other room, I heard the stereo. The Supremes. I turned a pale shade of red. I was busted. She heard my awful singing.

"Is that Diana Ross sitting in my kitchen drinking coffee?" She teased.

"No, it's a big dork who must learn to sing softer."

"Aw, it was cute. Next time do one I know, maybe we can work out a duet."

"Do you eat breakfast? I can make you something."

"I'll have one of those blueberry Pop-Tarts. They're my fave," she said. I beamed.

I brought her a toaster pastry and a cup of black coffee. She took one sip, looked repulsed then added a gallon of milk and a bag of sugar. Without looking up at me, she took my pen and proceeded to fill in spaces on the crossword. I was annoyed and amazed at the same time. I wasn't used to sharing my Sunday morning ritual, but then again, maybe with some help I could finally conquer *The New York Times*. Being an English professor doesn't mean you know who ran for president in 1904. How on earth did she know it was Parker?

"What's your favorite kind of cookie?"

"Yours," she grinned.

"Seriously, I need to know these things."

"Oatmeal. Low fat milk. Diet Coke. Wheat bread. What else?"

"How often do you call your family?"

"Mom, twice a month. Dad, rarely. Bro, once a week. You?"

"Depends on what's going on. I have no set pattern. My sister called me a lot, but I rarely talk to anyone since she . . ." My voice trailed off

"Ah, the twin connection. She'd call to keep in sync?"

"Yeah, I wish you could have met Amy." I wished I hadn't brought up her name.

She continued filling in spaces on the puzzle, sensing I didn't want to discuss my family. I couldn't tell if she was a morning person or not. In the past we usually lay in bed, drank coffee and fooled around. Living together was a huge adjustment. We had to adapt to a daily routine, rather than just packing excitement into our few precious moments. We used to joke that we'd get nothing done if we lived together. We proved that to be true yesterday. Today was a different story—we had a lot to do and couldn't procrastinate forever. I sat there staring at her while she counted spaces and erased my answers.

"Don't worry, lady. We will figure it all out eventually. We have all the time in the world. Stop staring at me, and finish this puzzle." She said without looking up.

"I know." I kissed her on the forehead and grabbed another pen.

We spent the next several hours pulling her possessions from boxes and placing them on shelves, hangers and in drawers. We really should have bought some furniture; most of her stuff would have to stay in boxes until we went shopping. I felt bad that my stuff was all unpacked and organized but it didn't seem to bother her. I worried that maybe she only wanted to feel temporary but I felt better when she said she wanted to paint her name on the mailbox.

"I forgot to tell you that I'm supposed to go to a poetry reading on campus this evening. I think I'm gonna skip it though, we have a lot to do."

"You're just chicken to show your lesbian face so soon after the outing," she kidded.

"That may be part of it. But I'd rather stay here with you tonight."

"Can I go with you?" she asked, sounding sad that I didn't offer.

"I guess. If you really want to." I was just embarrassed about her hearing my poetry. I wrote most of it while she was away, so it was a bit depressing.

"I really want to, but you have to show me your boobies first."

I ripped the snaps open on my denim shirt and flashed her my bra. She argued that viewing a black bra does not a booby flash make. I couldn't argue, I think I saw a similar proverb in a fortune cookie once. I walked over to the stereo, dug around for a CD, cranked the volume and pushed play. Then, I escorted her to the hardwood chair in the den, closed the mini blinds and began my dance. I pulled my shirt down over one shoulder, then placed it back. I followed suit with the other side. While doing the hula with my hips, I pulled the shirt off completely, swung it over my head a few times and threw it across the room. She giggled with enthusiasm and wished she had some dollars. I danced over to her chair, placed my legs on either side of her and unbuttoned my jeans, slowly—one . . . at . . . a . . . time.

I continued grinding my hips and leaned over, placing my chest in her face. She knew the rules—never touch the dancer. I stepped back a few paces and slid my jeans to the floor. Next I inexpertly attempted to pull them over my feet to no avail. I had to sit down for a second and pull them off—it was either that or trip myself. When I imagined the first time I danced for her, I didn't envision this outfit. I pictured garters, heels and a short skirt but this would have to do. I strolled back to the chair and stood with my back to her. I did a happy little butt shake for a few minutes while she oohed and aahed. Then I looked over my shoulder and watched her face as I unhooked my bra. More giggles of delight. I slid the bra over my arms and flung it at her and in one huge jump, I turned around to face her. I clumsily shook my hips and straddled her again. She reached up to help me remove my panties. I slapped her hand away. She tried the other hand. Again, I slapped. She laughed riotously. I placed my hands on my hips and rolled my panties down my legs. Then I balanced myself on her shoulder and pulled them off over my feet. I continued the hip motions and breast jiggle until the song ended. When it was over, she clapped, smiled her gorgeous smile, and gave me a standing O.

Despite hysterical fits of laughter, we managed to get most of her unpacking done. It took me an hour to recover from the mortification of my impromptu dance. She teased me incessantly until I threatened to cry and she only teased me four or five more times after that. We decided to order a pizza before we headed north to the college.

"You gonna tip the delivery guy with a little butt shake?" She ribbed.

"Only if he's here in less than thirty minutes."

We flipped a coin to see who would drive so the other could drink. I couldn't decide which was worse, reading the poems sober or having her hear them with a straight mind. Heads, I had to drive. I figured this meant I could probably squeeze in one or two Irish coffees at the beginning then drink regular coffee the rest of the night. It was probably better that I didn't get really toasted in front of my students anyway. She was delighted that I lost the coin toss.

"Yea! Now I can be obnoxious with your students and flirt with the teacher."

"I'm going to set you alone off to the side."

"If you don't let me have fun, I'll tell them about the little breast jiggle you did."

"Damn, you play rough. Okay, sit where you want, but keep it clean."

As we drove I pointed out the little landmarks I pass everyday. She was too hyper to care. I motioned as we passed my old apartment complex. She smiled and looked at me like I was the most boring person on earth. Sometimes I forgot what a nerd I was. A poetry reading was not going to make me look any cooler. I decided to shut up and turn up the music. We sang along to Incubus and Weezer. We rapped with Blondie. I opened the sunroof so she could enjoy the stars outside the city limits. We arrived at the bar near the campus, across the street from the Language Building. I had to run to my office for my notebook. I usually have the poems memorized but I was flustered tonight. She chose to run inside with me rather than wait in the bar alone. She had never seen my office before. It was kind of cool having her there.

"So this is where you mold young minds?" she asked.

"Their minds are already moldy by the time they get here."

"Nice office. I don't see my picture out," she accused.

"Look behind you." I pointed to a picture on the credenza. It was one we had taken on vacation the year before. She seemed impressed that I put it out.

"So, who do you tell people I am? Your sister?"

"No, I tell them you are the ambassador to Jamaica," I joked.

"Wow. Now that you've been outed, they will all think you are sleeping with an ambassador. Won't they be disappointed to find out I have a normal job."

"Don't worry, I'll just tell them you are a carnie."

"That'll work, although I prefer carnival employee."

I laughed as I headed to the door and flipped off the light. I thought she was right behind me. Instead she was sitting on my desk facing my chair.

"Ready? It starts in twenty minutes." I asked. She didn't move.

"You know, that's cool you have my picture out. I'm shocked." She seemed sad. She didn't look up at me when she spoke.

"Thanks, are you okay?" I whispered.

"What would you do if I asked you to eat me out on your desk?"

"Have a heart attack and never be able to concentrate at work again."

"Well, we wouldn't want that! Let's go wax poetic!" She was revved up again.

We walked into The Library and it was unusually packed for a poetry reading. I was surprised to see so many of my students there. Normally I'm lucky to get ten or twelve. Tonight almost every seat was filled around the stage and there were only a few stools at the bar. We bellied up, I ordered my Irish coffee and she got a whiskey sour.

"Full house tonight. You giving extra credit for attendance?" the bartender asked.

"No, I think they are here to ridicule me." I blushed.

"Well, we'd better get started before they get restless," he replied.

I put on my glasses and grabbed my drink and notebook. My companion looked a little nervous and a bit confused. I decided to go for broke tonight. I took her hand.

"You want to sit up front?"

"Can't I sit with you until you have to go up there?" she asked.

The bartender chimed in, "She runs the show, that's why her name is on the flyer. Didn't you know that?"

"No, it's news to me." She reddened. "You were gonna stay home for me?"

"I'd do anything for you, ya nut. Let's go." I led her to the front table and situated her between our new friend Emma and some exotic but harmless looking girl. They all shook hands and laughed. I climbed on stage and situated behind the microphone.

"Evening fellow poets. Let's make it good tonight. The ambassador to Jamaica has joined us." I winked. Everyone stared at her. She waved.

I started out by reading a few Dorothy Parkers and a short Whitman—a Whitman sampler so to speak. Then I introduced one amateur poet after the next. Some were confident and had some interesting work. Others were shy with shaky voices and weak rhymes. I didn't care. I didn't grade anyone tonight. Besides, my mind was on the looker in the front row. I was a little nervous when I introduced Emma. She told me earlier that she wrote one just for me and asked if she could read it. I told her to go for it.

"Next up, we have a very generous freshman, Emma Newton," I announced. And she read.

I am a student who works in a bar,
From the doctor's house, it isn't that far.
She came in last night,
With a beauty in white,
And now we all know what they are.

Everyone stared at me including my beauty in white. I felt obligated to respond or defend. I took off my glasses and approached the mike.

"Thank you Emma, I appreciate you're . . . um . . . candor. I don't normally appreciate limericks, but that one was very honest . . . the woman in white is a beauty."

Everyone clapped and looked incredulous. Then the girl in front requested that I recite. I made it a point to never argue with this woman, especially since my heart was in her hands. I wished I had prepared something more appropriate. In fact I was displeased with everything I brought with me. I fumbled through my notes looking for something upbeat. Then I realized I brought an old notebook. I guess I was distracted in my office. I had nothing good at all, just some crap from when I was lonely and suicidal. I hesitated.

"Okay, I've got two short ones and they both need work," I

stammered. Then I kicked myself. My number one rule when it comes to writing is never apologize for creativity. I put my glasses back on and leaned against the stool.

There is a place beside the ocean,
More beautiful than I dreamed.
There is a place inside the ocean,
Where all my tears have streamed.
The tears I cried
Have filled the ocean
And made the ocean blue.
These tears I cried came from my heart.
These tears I cried for you.

I received a round of polite applause. My beauty in white looked stunned but shot me an accepting smile. I was sure I'd catch shit on the way home for bad form, immature style and utter nonsense. But for now, she seemed supportive. I recovered and moved on.

The moon and stars fell from heaven
In a vibrant display of light.
The earth recovered but stayed in mourning
For the darkness of the night.

Given the reaction, I felt the need to apologize again. I wanted to explain that I didn't know whether it should read "morning" or "mourning." I wanted to describe how I was feeling when I wrote it. I wanted to get the hell back to the city immediately. Suddenly I realized how hard it must be for my students to get up there. Suddenly I wanted to change professions. Suddenly my beautiful girl smiled at me and everything was okay.

"I feel the need to recite one I wrote for her." I motioned at the lady in front and think I sounded a little nervous. She started clapping so I continued.

Sometimes I think of you
As the night trickles into morning.
I am still awake.
The vision of you

Dances in my mind
And plays with my imagination,
Wishing you were next to me
Telling me your dreams
As I live mine.

We stayed out too late. I know this because we were still in the bar at last call. People felt the need to come up and talk to me. I hate that. I don't like to get personal with students, especially when they are drunk. I managed to stay relatively sober, I only bypassed my Irish coffee limit by one and I finished it hours before we left. The whiskey sour drinker was not as conservative. She was on her fourth before the readings ended and ordered two more before we left. I saw a hangover in her future. I didn't say a word, as there had been too many nights where she poured me into bed. Besides, she was so friendly and happy and I enjoyed watching her interactions. I had to remind myself that she was closer in age to my students than she was to my own age.

We skipped to the car and headed south. I opened the sunroof while she groped for the CDs, trying to find the perfect song.

"You don't have anything good! What happened to all the ones I gave you?"

"I had them bronzed. What do you think? They are in the bedroom," I answered.

"Ah. So . . . that was fun tonight, eh? You freakin' yet?"

"No, I think I'll be okay. I'm glad you went with me though."

"Me too. I got three phone numbers and a hickey in the bathroom."

"And they say poets are boring people." I grinned.

"Thanks for reciting my favorite."

"Well, I felt I had to redeem myself after reading my others."

"Uh-uh. Did you give it a title yet?"

"No, I still call it 'A Poem for What's Her Name'."

We drove the rest of the way home in silence. She watched the stars through the sunroof and occasionally looked my way. I set the cruise control and put my hand on the back of her neck. She smiled at me and leaned to the left. I touched her cheek and took her hand. She squeezed it tight and changed radio stations.

"You know, you really are a big ol' dork."

"I know. But you want me anyway." I whispered.

"Damn straight!" she shouted and moved her hand to my thigh.

As we approached the off-ramp she was rubbing my thigh really hard.

"You want me to move my hand?" She asked.

"Yes, faster and to the left," I moaned. She laughed and behaved.

We got back to the house around one. She stumbled inside singing at the top of her lungs. I didn't bother to stop her. I thought it was funny. I would have joined in, but I couldn't quite figure out exactly what song she was singing. When we got inside I forced her to drink some water and take some aspirin. I got the coffee maker ready and set my alarm for five. When I crawled into bed, she was already settled. I double-checked her alarm clock and turned off the TV. I lay there thinking about the events of our first weekend together. It was pretty incredible. I hoped things would be that great forever. I was ready to fall into a rut with this woman. I was happy and I was in love. She let out a soft moan and moved closer to my side. I watched her sleep for about an hour then I wrapped my arms around her as tightly as I could.

"I love you," I whispered

She was fast asleep.

I felt like I had only been asleep for a few minutes when I heard my alarm go off. I hit the snooze button and rolled over to find a warm space in an empty bed. It took me a few minutes to remember that she was supposed to be next to me, which used to be a rare treat for a weekday. I sat up and called her name but got no response. I stumbled toward the bathroom tripping over empty boxes and broken glass. I found my beautiful delicate flower heaving into the toilet. I tend to be a sympathetic vomiter myself, but started laughing instead.

"It's not funny," she whispered through shivers.

"No, you're right. It's terrible. Maybe I should do an intervention. Better yet, given the vast amount of vomit, maybe I should do an exorcism."

She grabbed her head and started laughing. I felt awful that she was going to have to start her workweek with a hangover. I felt even worse that I didn't have time to nurse her back to health. I handed her a wet washcloth and headed out of the bathroom.

"Where are you going, my little enabler?" she asked through giggles.

"To the other bathroom, I have to pee."

"Okay, but one of these days I hope you will feel comfortable enough to pee in my presence." She had said this a million times.

"I will one day, but I won't ever feel comfortable enough to pee in your puke."

"Nice image. Thanks, I am feeling less embarrassed now."

I continued on with my morning routine, checking on her every few minutes. She had made her way back to bed and was flipping channels on the TV while fighting with the cat. I brought her some dry toast and black coffee. She looked at them with round eyes and turned a shade of green—not really kelly green, more of a pea soup green. When I returned a few minutes later, she was explaining to the cat why he should never start drinking. She told him all the awful side effects like hangovers, potential liver damage and chronic dehydration. He stared blankly at her for a few minutes then scurried out of the room. I giggled incessantly as I finished getting dressed.

"Hey, I gotta leave, I'm sorry."

"Enjoy your day. Don't worry about me," she said with a puppy pout.

"You'll be okay, just don't breathe on anyone." I'm so sensitive.

"Good advice. That explains why the cat ran off." She reached up for a kiss.

I gave her a slow, soft kiss and almost considered calling in sick. Then I remembered that I had outed myself over the weekend and realized that my absence would be interpreted as cowardice. She grabbed my ass and told me to get the hell out of there. Apparently her sensitive lover was headed over with juice and aspirin. I informed her that she needed an AA sponsor more than she needed another lover. A pillow met the back of my head as I headed out the door.

Chapter Ten

I made it through Monday with little embarrassment. No one really acknowledged my recent confession, although I got a few knowing glances and crooked smiles. I was well liked by the students and my sexuality was not unusual given the fact that I taught at Central Woman's University. It was rumored that the 16-story dormitory was pretty much a lesbian free-for-all. The rumor intrigued me and even gave me some exhaustive fantasies but I never made the attempt to confirm the tale for myself.

My alcohol-saturated lover made it through Monday with little embarrassment as well. She said she started feeling better after she showered, but the wave of nausea returned while riding the elevator up to her office. I asked her if she threw up again. She blushed and told me what she does in the privacy of her workplace is none of my concern. I told her to add barf bags to the grocery list. She told me to shove the grocery list up my ass. I liked our lighthearted rapport most of the time but sometimes I worried that her remarks were more honest than humorous. I decided to make sure she was still joking, so I grabbed the grocery list and lifted my skirt. She immediately left the room.

"Where are you going?" I insisted.

"To get you some lotion, you'll never get that up your ass without lubrication."

Okay, she was kidding. I made a mental note to pay attention to her inflection when she tells me to shove inert objects into my body cavities.

We decided to take a vote on what to do for dinner. Our options were limited due to lack of groceries. We narrowed it down to Chinese delivery, Pop-Tarts or the eclectic bistro down the street. The final tally was two for the bistro and one for Chinese—my kitty just loved sweet and sour chicken. I changed into some jeans and waited impatiently while my high maintenance beauty reapplied her make-up.

"Why are you getting all dolled up, doll?"

"You never know when you might run into the Pope," she quipped.

"Yes, I hear he likes to dine with lipstick lesbians."

"A guy's gotta eat."

We eventually made our way to the restaurant. She requested a table for two in the non-Pope section. The hostess sneered and led us to a table by the kitchen. I was never one to try new things, so we had a deal to take turns ordering for each other. I preferred the children's menu. She had a taste for the exotic. Tonight she ordered us French onion soup. I hated onions. For the main course she asked for rack of lamb. I despised the idea of eating lamb. She saw the look on my face and started laughing. She amended the order by requesting filet mignon instead. I nodded my head in approval.

"It's not like I ordered veal, Doc."

"True. But have you heard the expression gentle as a lamb?"

"Yes, have you heard the expression you are what you eat?"

"I am not even going to respond to that. Too many options."

Our soup arrived quickly and I put on my brave face and took a bite. We sat in silence slurping our onion concoction for several minutes. Suddenly my dining companion looked at me in terror.

"Wait a minute, you hate onions, don't you?"

I nodded.

"If you hate onions, then why are you eating the onion soup?"

"I hate onions but I love you. I've got priorities."

I glanced back down at my ugly brown liquid and felt her lips hit my forehead. I looked up and she kissed me long and deep, right there in front of the uninterested patrons.

"What was that for?" I asked when I regained my composure.

"No one has ever loved me enough to ignore their hatred for onions."

"I am allergic to strawberries. What do I get if I eat a few of those?"

"A trip to the emergency room and a disapproving look from the cat."

"Well, I wouldn't want to upset the cat. He might leave me." I grinned.

"He'd stay if you ate onion flavored cat food for him."

We slowly ate our steaks and lingered over dessert and coffee. W made small talk and asked questions that you would think we would have already asked over the past four years. We found out things about each other that were interesting or fun or flat out gross.

"What was the most embarrassing moment of your childhood?"

I thought for a moment, "There are so many, I can't settle on just one."

"Just give me the highlights."

"In the seventh grade I was asked to the Valentine's Day dance by the nerdiest guy in class. My mom made me go to be polite. I thought I would sneak in, stay a few minutes, get sick and have to go home. I figured no one would notice if I was there a short time. I wore one of my mom's silky see-through red shirts, which I didn't know was see-through. When the lights on the dance floor hit me just right, it almost appeared that I was topless. I didn't live that down for years."

"Couldn't you see the bra?"

"I didn't wear a bra until ninth grade, I was quite the late bloomer."

"You have those big boobies now and you didn't need a bra until you were fifteen?"

"I was an A cup until I was twenty-two, then the C cups showed up out of nowhere. Amy was a B cup since she was twelve. It was the only way people could tell us apart as twins. I didn't shave my legs until I was ridiculed by my basketball teammates in the eighth grade. I didn't even get my period until I was in high school. I was happy to postpone the girly stuff. I wanted to be a tomboy forever. Amy got everything early and hated it. I felt like she grew up faster than I and she hated that I didn't have to deal with all the puberty bullshit like she did. What's your moment?" I suddenly had a million things in my head and was dying to hear about her stories as well.

"You know I don't embarrass easily. I did go through an awkward age where everything hit me at once. I had braces, pimples, swollen bug-bite breasts and bad, bad hair. I felt like I had chronic body odor and my feet were very large for a girl of eleven. Every waking moment of every day for a year was a huge embarrassment for me. On top of all that, I was experiencing scary feelings of attraction toward some of my classmates. I wanted to play football with the boys on Saturdays but on Saturday nights I wanted to have sleepovers with the girls."

"Got any pictures?" I would have killed to see that.

"They were all destroyed, although my folks have a few family portraits that I could get my hands on. Look in the tack room next time we're at my parent's ranch."

I made a mental note to do so. "When did you discover that these scary feelings toward classmates meant that you were gay?" I loved a good coming out story.

"When I was a sophomore in high school I went to the Junior Symphony Ball with a few of the other rich kids. I shared a limo and a six-pack with two guys and a perky cheerleader. On the way to the dance, the two guys started mugging down, just very casually, like they did it all the time. The cheerleader and I stared in awe while we slammed our beer. I remember being scared and intrigued, I never knew that we were allowed to do that with our own gender. It seemed so beautiful and natural for them, so the girl and I leaned in and kissed each other. My palms got sweaty and my stomach sank. I thought I was in love. We kissed for about two minutes before she pushed me away and told me I was disgusting. I was miserable the rest of the night but knew that the two-minute kiss with her was better than any experience I'd had with a guy."

"You were hooked. And your first gay kiss was with a cheerleader. Figures. When did you tell your family?"

"I don't remember ever telling my family. I think Toby figured it out and probably informed mom and dad. It seemed very simple in my household, one minute I was dating boys and the next I was using the limo to go to gay bars. My parents have not been totally understanding, I know they are disappointed. They make their remarks, but they always welcome women into their home. The only big argument was when I wanted to take a girl to prom. My dad said that the press would find out and the Laine name would be soiled. That's when I realized that I needed to be discreet for the sake of the family business. What about you, Doc, when did you make the mammoth discovery?"

"I'd always known something was different about me. I never in a million years would have thought I was gay. I just hated changing clothes in the locker room and I was jealous of the guys who dated my friends. When I was a freshman in college, I met a girl in the dorm. We got along great and I followed her around like a loyal puppy. I used to write her notes telling her how cool she was and I never found it weird to pass notes to a girl in college. Apparently her mother found it weird. The girl stopped talking to me and told everyone in the dorms that I was a lesbian. I totally denied it and made a point to bring men home every night."

"So you became a slut with men to deny the fact that you were gay?"

"Pretty much. I've slept with more than my fair share of men. Anyway, a few weeks after my friend shunned me, I saw my phonetics teacher in a bar. I sat down next to her and ordered a beer. The bartender wouldn't accept my fake ID, so I got up to leave. I felt a hand on my shoulder and heard my teacher say, 'She's with me'. The bartender brought me beer after beer and we sat and talked for hours. Eventually the conversation led to boyfriends. I lied and told her I was seriously dating a guy. She laughed and said, 'gay women shouldn't date men, it's too confusing for everyone'. I insisted that I wasn't gay and she leaned in and kissed me. Like you said before—my palms got sweaty, my stomach sank and I thought I was in love."

"So what ever happened between you and the teacher?"

"Nothing, she was straight." I laughed.

"When did you tell your family?"

"Well, I think Jack had big brother instinct. He let me pal around with his friends and we would look at dirty magazines. I never flat out told him but about eight years ago he dropped in to say hi and found a woman in my bedroom. He was very cool about it and took us both out for breakfast."

"What about Amy, how did she react?"

"I never told her. I am sure she suspected. I don't know if Jack ever told her. I guess I'll never know if she knew." I suddenly wanted to go home.

"Doc, she probably knew and didn't care. You were twins, there is a chance that she was gay too, you know? How did your parents react?"

"I wondered a time or two if she was gay. I never felt the need to ask and Jack never mentioned anything to me, even after her death." I stared at my coffee, "I never told my parents. They think I am too busy to settle down and I don't think they would take it well. Hell, I married a man to live the dream for them."

"Okay lady, enough sharing for one night. It would take ten therapists and five years to sort though your family's dysfunction."

We paid the check and walked home in silence. I think she felt bad that we discussed Amy. I was feeling bad that she learned that my parents don't even know she exists.

Chapter Eleven

The next few months were uneventful. We exhausted ourselves at work and spent the evenings unpacking and organizing. We had our standard jocular repartee, we made love as often as possible and we made plans for the weekends. Our goal was to get up early one Saturday morning and finally buy some furniture and groceries. We had plans to hit the bars Friday night with some friends, so I predicted that getting up early meant ten or eleven o'clock.

We were an hour late meeting our friends Friday night because neither of us could seem to leave the shower. We arrived at the restaurant pruny and fulfilled. Our tardiness demanded redemption, so we vowed to hit every bar on the strip and dance until they said we could leave. The problem with having friends who are single is that they can dance all night and have no desire to go home until the cows come home. We went from one bar to the next, two-stepping one hour and swing dancing the next. We shot tequila and slammed Coronas. We found ourselves sandwiched between drag queens at one bar and between butch biker babes at the next. It was nearly four in the morning when we poured ourselves into a taxi.

When we finally arrived home after the cabbie had us lost for forty minutes, my brilliant drunk counterpart had the great idea of staying up all night rather than risking another hangover. I still wonder why stupid ideas make so much sense when you are drunk. We made a beeline to the Pop-Tarts and coffee pot. Bad news—only one Pop-Tart and less than a scoop of coffee. This struck us as really funny. We split the pastry and made four cups of really weak coffee. In my drunken stupor, I assumed that because the coffee was weak that it was also cold. The nice stain I left on my white shirt when I spit it out outdid the burn I sustained on my tongue. This struck us as really funny. We decided that perhaps a few more tequila shots would help us to get through the morning. We took several body shots each and even cracked open a few beers.

The last thing I remembered was the sound of cartoons coming from the extraordinarily loud TV. The first thing I encountered when I woke up on the kitchen floor was the smell of old coffee and a weird flashback to my freshman year of college when I mixed muscle relaxers with Keystone Light. I slowly managed to stand and look around for my partner in crime. She was lying face down on top of a coloring book. The cat was lying on top of her butt, taking a bath. This struck me as really funny. I think I was still drunk, yet it hurt to laugh. I checked her pulse just because I read once that you should do that. She was alive. I probably could have guessed that by the sound of her heavy snoring but I wanted to be sure. This struck me as really funny. Yup, I was still drunk.

I made my way to the bedroom and lay down. I had no intention of bringing my partner with me. I was afraid she would spew if I moved her. I glanced at the clock and was shocked to see what time it was. The digital display read 8:47. I ran to the window to see if this was a.m. or p.m. I was even more shocked to see that the sun was up. I was sure it was nighttime. I couldn't believe that I was able to stand after a few hours of sleep but I would have been more surprised if I were this hung over after sleeping all day. I decided to take advantage of my windfall of time, knowing that if I lay down I would be comatose all day. I dragged my tequila-soaked body to the shower and took my time getting dressed. I think I encountered some sort of time warp because when I finally got back out to the kitchen, the clock read 10:12. I must have stared at the shower wall for half an hour and didn't even realize it. Not surprisingly, my lady was still in the same position but the cat had stopped bathing and was now chewing on her hair.

It took me fifteen minutes to find my cars keys. The search for my car was even more time consuming. Eventually, I realized that we took a cab home and left my car downtown. That was a reassuring discovery—ten years earlier I would have found my car in the neighbor's flowerbed. I got the keys to her convertible and headed for the store. I returned with twelve bags of who knows what. I walked into the kitchen, bags overflowing, to find my coloring book queen AWOL. I searched the den, bedroom and bathroom. She was nowhere to be found. I asked the cat where she was. He shot me an incredulous glare. I heard a noise in the backyard and glanced out the window. I saw a very sexy, very sickly 25-year-old putting compost in a wheelbarrow. Next to her stood the appreciative old lady who lived next door.

It took us a few hours to finally get our shit together enough to function. We were able to sort out the groceries and piece together the sketchy details of the previous night/morning. What we couldn't figure out was how the patio furniture had been relocated into the dining room. The cat was no help whatsoever in explaining this phenomenon. We assumed that we figured we could save time shopping if we just used the furniture we already had on hand. Of course the obvious explanation was that we were just really, really drunk. Our extreme dehydration and craving for fried foods confirmed the latter theory.

We managed to make it to the furniture store later than we hoped. We prioritized the necessities since we only had a few hours until the stores closed. As we walked in, I made a beeline to the Art Deco and Retro furniture. She headed straight to the comfy, country styles. I knew already that we had a problem. I continued to browse knowing that if I went to find her I would be easily swayed. All she had to do was smile at me and I would give in. I wanted to hold my ground on this; our house was a Thirties renovation and I had painted it with bright colors and retro patterns. I refused to buy furniture that belonged at a bed and breakfast. As I stared at a red leather sofa, my cell phone rang.

"Hello?"

"Mmmm, yes, I am taking a survey . . . you aren't seriously interested in that monstrosity of a sofa, are you?" She asked this sounding very concerned.

I looked around and didn't see her anywhere.

"Mmmm, yes, as a matter of fact, I am very interested. I like the lines and the color would look great with a rug my partner gave me for Christmas."

"I see. So, do you like it, do you really, really like it?"

I finally spotted her smiling at me from behind an armoire. I stared at her while I spoke.

"The more I look at it, the more I love it."

"Well, if you love it so much, why don't you marry it?" She laughed.

I kept staring at her.

"Is that how it works? If you love something you have to marry it?"

She stared back intently.

"Yes, I do believe that's how it works." She sounded serious.

"Even if marrying a sofa isn't legally accepted in the United States?" I asked.

"Then that makes the act of doing it even more symbolic and selfless." She stepped out from behind the cabinet and inched closer to me.

"Do you think the sofa would have me?" I was feeling a little faint.

"I bet if you asked it nicely, it might say yes."

She walked up next to me and turned off her cell. I did the same. She had tears in her eyes and I felt a lump form in my throat.

"I have been in love with you since the moment I heard your name," I began through tears. "I have never had so much fun, felt so much passion nor been so happy." My voice shook. "Everyday has been a beautiful adventure. I can't imagine my life without you. You make me strong, you are my muse, my best friend, my family and my future." I was practically bawling. "If you can put up with me for the rest of our life, then I would be honored to marry you."

"Are you asking me or merely stating a fact?"

God, she could be difficult at times. She never let me off the hook easily.

"Dreamer, will you marry me?"

"No. It's not legally recognized and I know you think it's a waste of effort."

I admit part of me was a little relieved. I did feel that way several years ago before I met her. I was married to a man for many years so I had done the ceremony and wifey-thing already. On the other hand, I did sort of feel like a commitment ceremony would ensure our future together. I tried not to look disappointed and I kind of felt stupid for asking.

"Hey"—she took my hand—"every girl wants the ceremony once in her life. I know you already had yours but I would kind of like to know what it feels like to have the 'rite' even if it's not our right." She mimed quotation marks with her fingers. "So, ask me again. Better yet, I'll ask you. Will you marry me?"

I squeezed her hand, "Yes, I will."

Forgetting where we were, I instinctively leaned over to kiss her. Out of nowhere, a salesman approached and cleared his throat.

"So, ladies, what do we think of the sofa?"

"We'll take it!" We shouted in unison. We had to buy it. It was a red leather monstrosity of an engagement ring.

We picked out a few other items to go with the symbolic sofa. I was delighted that she gave in to my wishes on the style although I could tell she was a bit disappointed. I made a deal with her that she could choose the furniture for the guest rooms, sun room and what was left in our bedroom. She decided she would probably peruse some antique stores, which thrilled me to no end. I was permitted to design the kitchen, living room and office. The compromise thing was working out great.

We left the furniture store giddy with excitement, we had so many things to plan. A day of hangover turned into a day of mapping out our life together. As we climbed into her little sports car, she was singing Motown at the top of her lungs. She did this a lot and I usually either blushed or sang along. Today, I sang along.

"So, where do you want to have this little ceremony?" she asked between verses.

"Well, if it's just us, we could go back to Holland like we did last year. But if you want to make it a public affair, we could do it at the hotel."

"That's a little too public with the press and all." She seemed annoyed that I even brought it up. She was already in the papers a lot for being heir to the Laine fortune, owning the hotel and signing on to the biggest law firm in town. When it got out about her homosexuality, we spent weeks avoiding the press. I could understand why she didn't want to make a big deal about a ceremony.

"We are just doing this for us, right?" she quizzed.

"Absolutely. I'll take the summer off and we can go back to Amsterdam. Can you take some time off from the firm?" I already knew the answer was no.

"Well, it's doubtful, but I might be able to take a week if the Rogers' case doesn't end up going to trial." She seemed optimistic. "Shall we invite our families? At least it will give them a little vacation. I know my brother would love Holland."

"Yes, sex and drugs. Toby would be right at home there," I teased. He was in the press quite a bit as well.

We came to a stoplight and she turned and stared at me. I said nothing. She drove a few more blocks in silence with her eyebrows furrowed.

"Hello? Gonna answer my question? Want to bring your family."

"You know the answer to that already." I knew this would be an issue one day.

"You are divorced, over thirty and the head of a college English department. I think you are grown up enough to tell your parents that you are a lesbian." She was livid.

"I know," I sighed and looked out the window.

"Doc, you don't think they actually believe that you moved sixty miles from your job to get a roommate, do you?" She was ready to argue. "And you can't expect your sweet brother to keep covering for you. Jack has told me a hundred times that your parents already suspect it. At least help your bro out so he doesn't have to lie for us."

"I'll figure it out." I was watching an ice cream truck surrounded by kids.

"One more thing, Grumpy, we have been together for years you know. Don't you want to share your happiness and new world with your parents? Your brother has really enjoyed the parties, trips and hotel perks. He is totally fine with it and he loves and accepts me, I am sure your folks will be the same way."

I didn't know how to respond. I was supposed to be happy and all of the sudden I was remembering the day I told my parents I was getting married the first time. I cried when I told them. They thought they were tears of joy. In reality, they were tears of shame. I knew I was gay back then. I should have told them then.

"Don't you think they wonder why you take your ex-husband to your family reunions? Don't they wonder why you and your ex couldn't make the marriage work yet you remain best friends to this day? Why when they come south do they stay with him?"

I sat there watching the ice cream truck drive away as the kids chased it.

"Baby, you have been a part of my family's lives ever since the first night you met my brother and me. You have been to my parent's house for holidays, for birthdays and you have traveled all over the world with my family. You have become a member of my family."

"So what are you saying? That it is a bigger sacrifice for you since your family owns half the city?" I have no idea where that came from.

"What? No! I am saying that today we decided to share a life together forever, yet you won't even let me meet your parents. You held my hand at my grandmother's funeral. I couldn't even call you at the hospital the day your twin sister died much less attend her funeral with you." She was shouting. "Who held your hand at Amy's funeral?"

I didn't respond.

"Who held your hand, Doc?" she screamed.

"Steve." I started crying.

"That's right, Steven. You gave your sister's eulogy holding hands with your ex-husband and his pregnant wife. I spent the worst day of your life on standby at LAX praying that you would call and ask me to come home to you." Her voice softened. "You know, you never even shed a tear in my presence. You cried to your brother, you went and stayed with your parents for a week. You never even talked to me about how you felt when your own twin died."

I was speechless. I didn't know she was at LAX all day. I didn't know she was holding all this inside about Amy's death.

We pulled up at the house and both went inside without saying a word. I sat down at the kitchen counter and put my head down. I felt her come up behind me and touch my back while she placed some objects on the counter. I looked up and saw a bottle of tequila, a frozen pizza and the telephone. I turned around to see what she was up to. She didn't even look back at me as she grabbed her car keys and walked out the door. I knew what she meant for me to do and I couldn't do it. I sat at the counter and cried.

Eventually my tears subsided and I started thinking about the situation. Of course I needed to tell my parents and include my partner in my family. If the tables were turned, I would probably be furious if she excluded me. I think it made a huge difference that her parents lived in the same city and mine were thousands of miles away. It made it easier for me to hide and lie because my parents rarely visited. It also made a difference that she was in the public eye and I was just a little schoolteacher at a small, Southern woman's college. Still, I knew she was right and that I had to quit rationalizing why the circumstances were different. I knew I had to make things right.

I put the pizza back in the freezer and poured a tequila shot. A little courage couldn't hurt. I took one whiff of the liquor and almost threw up. The alcohol of the night before was still in my body. I didn't think I would ever be able to drink tequila again so I poured the shot in the sink and made some coffee. My hands were shaking and I felt faint. I needed a cigarette. I hadn't smoked in ages but there was usually a pack lying around, leftover from a party. I located a crushed pack of menthols and sat back down at the counter. I lit the stale cigarette, took a long, wonderful drag and reached for the phone.

"Mom?" My voice shook.

"Hey, stranger. What's shaking?" She sounded chipper.

"Well, if you have a minute, I'd like to talk to you."

"Is everything okay? Jack, Ste—"

"Everyone's fine," I interrupted her. "Mom, I need to tell you something."

"Okay. Shoot."

The tequila was looking better and better. I reached for the bottle and took a huge swig. It rolled down my throat and I gagged. I took another drag of my cigarette and choked.

"Honey, are you okay? What do you want to tell me?"

"I'm okay. Mom, I'm gay."

Silence.

"Mom, did you hear me? Are you still there?"

"I'm here. I heard you." She sighed.

I wanted to hang up the phone and curl up in the fetal position.

"Sweetie, I know you are gay."

"How long have you known?" I wanted to kill my brother, the traitor!

"I've known since you were about twelve. I probably knew before you did."

"Why didn't you say anything?"

"Sweetie, it's not up to me to out you. You make your own choices. When you married Steve, we figured maybe we were wrong in our assumption. When you divorced him we thought maybe that was the reason. It was the only reason we could come up with. You still love each other so much and all."

"So you are okay with this?"

"To be honest, your father and I have mourned over it for years. We've grieved the loss of our dreams for you. We've cried over your past struggle and the struggle you will always have. We're not okay with this. It's been a hard thing to accept and now that you've told us, we'll need more time to adapt to the changes we'll encounter now."

"I'm so sorry, Mom."

"Are you happy though?"

"I'm happy. I'm in love. Sh—"

"The socialite?" I was interrupted. "Your dad has some friends who saw you two dancing at some AIDS benefit a year or so ago."

"Yes, she's the one." I felt so proud to admit it.

"How long have you been with her?"

"A little over three years now."

"You have loved someone for three years and not shared one detail of her existence with us? Is she the roommate you moved to the city for?"

"Yes. We decided today to have a Unity ceremony this summer."

I think I shared too much for one day. My mother fell silent.

"Mom, are you there?" I panicked.

"Let's do this a little at a time. I will call you tomorrow."

She hung up. I sat there for an eternity and stared at the phone. When I accepted the fact that she wasn't going to call me back, I took the cigarettes, some Coronas and the Cuervo bottle and moved to the den. The cat followed me in and curled up on my feet. I had downed three beers when I heard the front door open. Neither the cat nor I got up.

"Kitty! Doc! Where you at?"

"In the den." My voice was raspy from smoking and crying.

"It reeks in here! Kitty, are you smoking?" She seemed happy. She walked into the den fanning the air and pretending to cough.

"Kitty always smokes when he comes out to his parents," I quipped and couldn't help but smile.

"You did it? Oh my God! Tell me everything!" She skipped to the sofa and cracked open a beer.

"There's not much to tell. She said she already knew I was gay. She asked about you. I told her our plans and she basically hung up."

"Oh." My partner looked crestfallen. "I am so sorry, baby."

"Yeah. Me too." My eyes welled up with tears.

"Are you okay?" She leaned toward me.

"I'm fine." I hated being vulnerable.

"Really?" She started to cry.

I don't know where it came from. Maybe it was the alcohol, the marriage proposal, the talk of Amy or my mom's disappointment. For the first time in our relationship, I completely lost it. I laid my head in her lap and sobbed. I cried so hard that I couldn't breathe. She stroked my hair and I could feel her crying along with me.

We were both finally starting to calm down when my phone rang. We just stared at each other. I knew I couldn't talk to anyone right now, but I was anxious to see if it was my parents. She answered the phone on the third ring. She never answered my phone before in case it was my folks. I heard her voice lower and I couldn't detect what she was saying.

"Hey, Steven's on the phone. I told him what happened. I am sure you will want to use his shoulder tonight."

"Can you tell him I will call back tomorrow?" I whispered.

"You don't want to talk to him?"

"No, tonight I want to talk to you."

She grinned and danced back to the kitchen. She sounded ecstatic when she told him what I said. I think he completely understood. I heard her say, "I know! It's about freakin' time!"

She came back into the den with some tissues and a bag of peanuts.

"Did you eat?" She asked.

"No, I'm not hungry though, thanks." My voice was still raspy.

"Doc, are you really okay? You never turn down food." She looked nervous.

I took one look at her worried blue eyes and started crying again. My heart jumped when I realized how much I needed her and how much I loved her. I wept.

"Shhhh. Baby, it's okay." She stroked my hair.

I wanted to talk, but the tears kept coming. Again, I couldn't catch my breath. She adjusted herself underneath me and we both got comfortable. I never cried so hard or for so long in my life. At a few points I was hysterical and hyperventilating. She calmed me down and got me to breathe. Every emotion I had felt over the last ten years surfaced. I lay in her arms for hours. I drifted in and out of memories and in and out of tears.

"Baby, tell me what you are thinking."

"I'm not sure. Everything. It's too much."

"I've known you three years and you have never actually cried. You saw your dad get sick, your husband remarry; you lost two cats and your twin sister. You never cried once in front of me. Doc, tell me what's going on."

"Just hold me tonight."

"Doc, please talk to me. I love you, you know that right?"

I wanted to talk. I really tried. Nothing came out but tears. No matter how hard I tried to get closer to her, I couldn't get close enough. No matter how hard I tried to talk, nothing came out but tears.

"Baby, let's go to bed." She stood and reached for my hand.

I slowly got up. My body was sore, my head was pounding. I took her hand and she led me to the bedroom. I stood at the foot of the bed not knowing what to do. I watched her set my alarm then she walked over and unbuttoned my shirt. I just stared at her blankly. She removed all my clothes except my panties then pulled a clean T-shirt over my head. She guided me to the bed and helped me lie down. She pushed my hair back and kissed my forehead. I watched her disappear for a few minutes to lock up the house. She returned, took off her clothes and crawled into bed next to me. The minute her body touched mine, I began crying.

"Baby, talk to me. I want to know everything."

"Can you just hold me tonight?"

She tightened her embrace and I felt safe. I still couldn't get close enough to her though. I cried myself to sleep feeling her cry along with me.

Sunday morning I woke up exhausted. I remembered that she had set the alarm so we could go to our monthly brunch. When I glanced at the clock, I saw that it was almost nine, way too late to make it on time. I didn't have much recollection of the previous night. Bits and pieces came to me like a bad dream. It wasn't that I was drunk the night before, I was just overwhelmed with emotion. I don't recall ever having that kind of emotional outburst in my life. It made me wonder if maybe I was a cold person with an indifferent soul. I always told myself that I was merely independent and emotion was for people who needed to be taken care of. It struck me a little that morning that maybe I needed to be taken care of once in awhile.

The house seemed very quiet. I figured that my counterpart must have gone to the brunch without me. I was okay with that as I was slightly embarrassed about my behavior in front of her. I turned on the TV hoping to find something mindless on MTV. I was in luck—the Real World Marathon had just begun. I situated myself for a long day of recovery when my partner danced into the room with coffee and doughnuts.

"Good morning, Angel Butt!" She must have had a lot of coffee already.

"I thought you might have gone to the brunch." My voice was still crackly.

"Without my mate? Never!" She handed me a cup and filled it.

Her smile was incredible. She seemed so confident and happier than normal. She stroked my hair and straightened my pillow. When the cat came in and sniffed the doughnuts, she shooed him away with a high-pitched rooster cackle.

"You're in an awfully good mood. Did you win the lottery?"

"Nope. I just had a great night." She beamed.

"I see, did you sneak over to your lover's after I fell asleep?"

"Nope. I am just in the afterglow of feeling your love."

I looked at her like she was nuts. I was slightly irritated that my sadness made her happy. "You act like I've never needed you before," I accused.

"I don't know that you ever have." She softened. "We have made love a thousand times and I don't ever think I have felt as close to you as I did last night. It wasn't just the emotional closeness I felt from you, which was a first and very nice. But you just never held me so close physically. In the middle of the night you wrapped your entire body around me so tightly that I actually had to ask you to loosen your hold."

"I don't even remember that."

"You were sleeping really hard."

She arranged the coffee pot on the nightstand, pulled off her robe and crawled back into bed. I rolled over to face her and the cat curled up between us.

"So, what do you want to do today?" she whispered. "Your wish is my command, anything your fragile heart desires."

"The crossword."

She reached under the bed and pulled out the Sunday *New York Times*, a pen and my glasses.

"Aren't you handy? Thanks." I took the paper and sat upright. I worked on the crossword for about half an hour while my beautiful girl watched me.

"Doc," she took my hand, "do you want to talk about anything?"

"Nah, I'm okay." I knew if I started talking I would cry all day. I laid the paper on the floor and rolled back over to face her.

"What can I do to make you feel better?"

"Make love to me." I blushed.

"Are you sure you want to right now?"

I started crying. I have no clue why. Maybe it was her kindness and my feeling of being vulnerable. She took my glasses from my face and set them on the side table. Slowly she climbed on top of me and lay there like a human blanket.

We made slow, passionate love way into the afternoon. Finally, I felt like I could get close enough to her.

Chapter Twelve

"The day is still relatively young. What do you want to do?" She shouted over the running shower while I brushed my teeth.

"I don't know. Something fun. Let's go to Vegas." I was actually serious.

"I thought of that, it's always been a good spontaneous distraction for us. But as I recall, tomorrow is Monday." She turned off the water. "But you have Spring Break in two weeks, we could go somewhere then."

"I thought you had a ton of work."

"Well, it occurred to me last night when I left you to call your mom that maybe I work too much and don't give enough time to our needs." She stepped out of the shower. "So I called Bobby last night and asked him to take over my new case so I could have your spring break off."

"You did that for me? You've only been at the firm a few

months. You'll lose your job." I was delighted but felt guilty for being so selfish.

"It's okay. I think my job is safe seeing as how they like using my name to get new clients. It's amazing what a little press will do for a law firm. Did you know that they picked up more gay clients in one week than in all their years combined after word got out that the socialite lesbian lawyer worked there?"

"I told you that might happen."

"You were right as usual, Smarty. Hey, I know what we should do today! Let's go crash a reception."

"What's going on there this afternoon?" I was excited. We hadn't done it in ages.

"Mmmm, I think it's a wedding reception. I'll call and find out."

"Anything but another bar mitzvah." We crashed one once and spent the whole afternoon dancing with horny teenage boys. I still had nightmares of a squeaky-voiced adolescent male grabbing my ass and trying out several awful pick-up lines.

"It's a fortieth anniversary party." She smiled as she hung up the phone.

"Yay!" We both started jumping up and down like hyper puppies. The anniversary parties were our favorite. You usually got a large group of retirees who had nothing better to do than get drunk and show pictures of their grandchildren. We liked to dance with the old men and flatter their wives.

"Shall we go sexy or conservative this time?" I was giddy.

"We don't want to give anyone a heart attack, let's try sexy conservative. We'd better hurry though, it starts in an hour and you know they never last very long when it's the senior citizen set."

We both ran to the closet, shoving the other out of the way. I knew she would try to grab my black tank dress I bought at a Nordstrom close-out a few weeks earlier. I was right, she beat me to the closet and already had the dress in hand by the time I rounded the corner of the walk-in.

"I don't think so Cinderella," I giggled and grabbed for the dress.

She released the dress with a fake sob and bowed her head. She put her arms behind her back and with head down, started to skulk out of the closet.

"Oh, all right, you can wear it—just this once." I handed her the dress.

"No, that's okay," she said in her best little girl voice. "I can just wear a burlap sack and some flip flops." She handed the dress back to me while batting her eyelashes. It was the flip flop reference that got me. I was dying to wear the dress but remembered that I didn't have any shoes to go with it. A bar mitzvah guest ruined my black pumps in a punch fiasco. We could wear the same size dress, but when it came to pant length and shoe size, I had her beat by a mile.

"I'll make a deal with you, you can wear the tank dress if you have the hotel send a car." I loved the hotel limo—a white stretch with a full bar and amazing stereo.

"Hmmm, that sounds like an unfair trade. I get the dress, the ride and a chance to get drunk on a Sunday." She considered the proposition just as the doorbell rang. "Oops, the limo's here, gimme my dress."

She beat me to the punch and I felt swindled. I wandered aimlessly through the closet until I finally stumbled on a red spaghetti strapped, lacy dress. Fifteen minutes later I was in the limo on my way to the beautiful Laine hotel. My drop-dead gorgeous partner and I had three shots and two beers along the way. By the time we arrived, we were primed and ready for fun. Unfortunately we had forgotten the gift for the anniversary couple. Major faux pas. I brilliantly stole a bottle of Dom from the limo and tied it to a rose lifted from the hotel lobby.

When we arrived in Ballroom C, the party was already underway. A string quartet was playing, people were dancing and no one batted an eye as we entered. We left the Dom on the gift table and found seats at a small table that the staff added when they saw us arrive. I grabbed us each a Heineken and we did our best to blend. As I wandered the room, I saw a few familiar faces, then spotted my partner's parents. I said my hellos and was informed that an old family friend was throwing this surprise anniversary party for his wife. That explains the familiar faces, so many I had seen at their family functions over the years.

Just as I was returning to our table, the host asked me to dance. He was a distinguished man who smelled of beer and Old Spice. I could hardly decline. He took my hand and led me to the center of the dance floor.

"Nice party, hope you don't mind us crashing," I said and blushed.

"I'm thrilled you are here, it was such a last minute affair, I didn't have time to invite everyone I should have." He couldn't dance and talk, my toes were already injured.

"Well, happy anniversary. It's quite a milestone."

"Thank you. I guess in forty years the Laines will be celebrating this anniversary as well."

I was a little confused, surely it hadn't gotten out about our pending marriage idea already.

"Is there a Laine wedding planned?" I was annoyed.

"There better be, I started working up the prenup for it yesterday."

My heart fell and I felt nauseated. I had no idea that she could be so fast to protect her fortune. I excused myself from the dancing lawyer and bolted straight to a cab and headed home.

I arrived back at the house more livid than when I first heard the word "prenup." The very phrase echoed in my head until it made no sense. I kept thinking maybe I heard wrong, maybe he meant he was going to "preen up" the trees at the Laine house. Suddenly it became laughable. Preen up, that's it, preen up: to prune or primp. I sat on the kitchen floor smoking another stale menthol and sipping a warm Corona. The combination of the two mixed with the nausea of the situation made me vomit. After a few rounds of "sicking up" in the sink, I collapsed on the cold ceramic tile floor. I'm not sure how long I was out but I was awakened by my concerned former fiancé. She was whispering my name and stroking my back. I slowly opened my eyes, saw her beautiful face and started weeping uncontrollably.

"What is it? Baby, what's wrong, why did you leave the party?"

I was on emotional overload after the past twenty-four hours and couldn't have responded even if I wanted to.

"Dreamer, talk to me." She tried again while putting cold water on a washcloth. I stopped crying and just stared at her. I had no idea where to begin. All I wanted to do was pack up my clothes and kitty and leave the only house I ever loved.

"Please just tell me something. Are you sick? Are you in pain?"

"I'm fine. Please just leave me alone." I stared at the floor.

"Are you in pain, are you hurt, what is it? I'm worried," she begged.

I pulled myself up to the counter and reached for my car keys. I had no idea what to do, I had never been sickened by her before much less ready to leave. I panicked and threw my keys at the microwave and ran to the bedroom. She didn't follow. I was both relieved and disappointed. Before I knew it I had two bags packed and I had no clue what was in them. I stalled a little on the toiletries hoping she would come in and beg me to stay. When I realized she wasn't coming near me, I finished throwing my things together, set my bags by the front door and went to find my keys. She was in the den watching TV. Nice, real concerned. I looked everywhere and couldn't find my keys.

"Lose something?" She called from the next room.

I felt so foolish having thrown them, I didn't want to admit I couldn't find them.

"No, I'm fine." I shouted back, probably louder than necessary.

"I'll make a deal with you, Doc—you tell me what's wrong and

I'll tell you where your keys landed."

It struck me at that moment that I wasn't sure what was wrong. Was I mad because she told people about our marriage plans? She might have been excited and anxious to share, that's understandable. Was I mad about the prenuptial agreement? She had every right to protect her family fortune. I rationalized, of course, that if gay marriage isn't legal, then no document protecting a gay partner would ever be necessary. What did I know, I didn't study law, I was just a stupid professor at a small women's college. She was the legal genius who graduated law school at twenty-three. Was I irked because our plans weren't even finalized before she had our demise prepared? Honestly, I don't know why I was mad. I decided it was because the idea of a prenup meant that she didn't trust me or didn't have faith that our "marriage" would last forty years. Suddenly I felt a little foolish and very, very scared.

"Tell me where my keys are and I will never burden you with my little life again."

Silence. She said nothing and I heard the channels change. This infuriated me even more.

"That's nice. I am on the verge of leaving you forever and you are channel surfing."

I heard her slam the remote on the coffee table and she tiptoed to the kitchen.

"Your keys fell behind the fridge. I'm blocking you in though, I can move my car or you can take the Jeep from out front."

Why wasn't she stopping me? Did she want this to happen. Was I set up?

"I'll take the Jeep, I wouldn't want you to be inconvenienced."

"What the hell is that supposed to mean? What is up your ass?" She was pissed.

I stood there for what seemed like forever. I practiced my answer in my head before I said it aloud.

"Frank Bonner said he was writing up a prenup. You know damned well that you can trust me. I paid for half this house, half the house in Jackson. I bought Mustang Sally and my car. I can't believe you would assume anything, especially so soon. We have been engaged all of twenty-four hours and haven't even told our friends yet." It all rushed out so quickly, I wasn't even sure it was coherent. She stood there beaming at me with a crooked smile. She didn't say a word.

"I'm not leaving you because of the prenup, I am leaving you because you didn't discuss anything with me first. I am leaving because you assume failure and we haven't even booked a flight yet."

Still, she just stood there with a grin on her face. She leaned toward the den and glanced at the TV.

"That's fine, jackass, just watch TV. I will go and you can have your perfect TV night."

She looked at me then glanced back at the TV. I heard a Hyundai ad and almost cried again. She looked at the clock, approached me and took my hand.

"I'm not going anywhere with you until you say something."

"Trust me."

"Trust you? You don't seem to trust me." I was shaking.

I gave in, she led me to the den and carefully placed me on the hard wooden chair directly in front of the big screen. She sat on the floor next to me and turned up the volume. The car commercial ended and went to a milk ad. I sat in silence, watching the flickering TV light bounce off her beautiful profile. She turned up the volume a little more as the commercials ended and the network went to "MTV News."

The veejay began, "Is it wedding vows for Amelia? Sources say that she eloped with Dallas trendsetter Tobias Laine. Laine is son to hotel mogul Arthur Laine and mystery writer Anna Laine." She continued, "Amelia Garcia, one of the most adored Latina musicians, may be off the market. Sorry fellows. Neither party could be reached for confirmation. Amelia's manager says that the two have been together a short time but decided to take the plunge last week."

I was speechless and she didn't say a word. She muted the TV and stared straight ahead.

"Wow, Toby got married?" I asked with a squeaky voice.

"So it seems."

"Did you know he was even dating her?" I was still squeaky.

"I honestly had no clue until he called my cell phone a few hours ago. Mom and Dad didn't even know. He has been gone for a month or so and we all assumed he was on another party binge in London. He's in Vegas until Thursday, then back here for an impromptu reception at the hotel."

"Amelia's a hottie. Good for Toby. I can't believe he settled down."

"I can't believe you freaked."

God, I felt so stupid. I wanted to crawl into a hole, instead we crawled into bed. Whew.

Chapter Thirteen

I slept hard and actually felt rested when I woke up Monday morning. I lay in bed for a few minutes before getting up to bask in the fact that I was still in love and still living in our amazing home. I looked around the room and saw the art and knickknacks we acquired over our years together. Then something struck me funny. I could literally *see* them, it was light in the room. My alarm was set for five, so it was supposed to be dark when I got up.

"Aaaaargh! Fuuuucccking!" I screamed and glanced at the clock. 8:42.

I overslept almost four hours? That was impossible. I had two alarms and the coffeepot set. I took a deep breath—no, no smell of coffee. I pulled the covers over my head and soccer kicked my legs.

"This is a nightmare, this is a nightmare . . . the last two days have just been a nightmare. Today is only Sunday." I was almost in tears.

I regained my composure and turned on the TV. "Good Morning America" was on. Shit.

"Son of a bitch! Aaaarrrggghhh!" I screamed again, scaring the cat.

"Oh my gawd! She's alive and pissed!" Someone shouted from the kitchen. The someone, of course, was my partner in crime who was also apparently late for work.

"What the hell is going on?" I shouted back. "Is it Groundhog Day?"

"I got you babe—now come here, woodchuck-chucker." She caught the movie reference. She was seated on the kitchen floor surrounded by my personal boxes from the attic. The sight was quite adorable. Kitty was weaving in and out of boxes and my sweetie was wearing a cowboy hat, cowboy pajamas, bunny slippers and a green wool scarf. I couldn't help but laugh.

"Why am I home when it's daylight on a Monday? Why aren't you at work? Why are you going through those bullshit boxes of useless crap? Why don't I smell coffee? Did you feed the kitty?"

"Wow. You sure curse a lot and ask a lot of questions. Kitty is fed, I will make a fresh pot in a minute, the boxes are full of wonderful stories and poetry written by my favorite author, I didn't have anything major to do today, and you called in sick."

I stood there dumbfounded. She answered all my questions, in reverse order, but I liked all the answers. I walked to the fridge and poured some orange juice.

"Oh." I said with a feeling of relief. "Did I really call in sick?"

"You played dueling alarm clocks all morning and seemed to have no intention of getting up. I got tired of your crawling over me to hit snooze, so I turned off the alarms and got up. I called your secretary at seven thirty and told her you were sick. Did you know that you have only called in sick twice in the past four years?"

"Yes, and both times were because you dragged me off for a

three-day weekend. What did she say about my not being there today?"

"She said you deserved a day or two and the TA will be so thrilled to actually have something to do. Apparently you are too efficient and have to do it all yourself. Frankly, I think they are delighted to be rid of you for a few days." She dumped unlevel scoops into the coffee maker.

"To be honest, I am thrilled to be off. I feel like I am losing my mind and I am totally burned out on teaching unappreciative illiterates."

"Maybe you should quit your job and do something creative. Don't you ever wish you'd pursued your dreams of being a hippie artist/poet/bum?" She held up some papers.

"You already have one author in your family. Have you already forgotten MTV's reference to your hotel mogul father and mystery writer mother?"

"Yeah. How funny is that? She writes one short story for an anthology and suddenly she's a writer. I guess it sounded better than saying 'Laine's martini-drinking mother'."

"I've considered quitting and trying something new. I know the cliche 'those who can't—teach'. I have always feared that I was a pure example of a washed-up writer-wannabe who taught college English to avoid being the next female Stephen King."

"Argh, Stephen King. He wouldn't even get a B in your class. Don't sell yourself short, you could be the next Judy Blume." She winked.

"Are you there, God? It's me, the overly dramatic lesbian." I laughed.

"All I am saying is that you will never know if you don't try." She wasn't laughing.

"I am proud of how far I have gone in such a short time. I would hate to give all that up and have to start at the bottom at a new college if I couldn't make the literary cut." I poured a cup of coffee and pondered a stale menthol.

"If you must smoke, there is a fresh pack in the freezer. I've been tempted myself so I keep a stash." She grabbed the frozen Marlboro pack and tossed it at me. I wish I had known earlier.

I opened the pack and lit one up without responding. It was delightful, comforting and so much better than the Salems I had smoked the past two days. Suddenly I had to excuse myself. When I returned from the bathroom she started in on me again.

"Doc, I know you worked hard but I know you will be successful at everything you do."

"I couldn't financially afford to even take a short sabbatical leave much less quit entirely."

I knew what was coming. After yesterday's prenup fiasco I really didn't want to have this conversation. I refused to give her all the money responsibilities, no matter how many hotels she owned.

"Why not just take the summer off. Don't teach any classes. Let Gregor act as department head for a few months. He held that job for thirty years before he went a little nutty, he can handle three months. You won't be out a paycheck that way. Plus, you know you never need to worry about money." She looked a little nervous with the last remark.

I glared at her for a second. She looked down at the cat and rolled her eyes. She probably expected a fight and I thought about giving her one. Instead I decided to ask questions first before making assumptions.

"Hey, madame. Are you gonna want a prenuptial agreement like Toby?"

"Hate to be the bearer of shocking news. The prenup wasn't for Toby, it was for Amelia. Frank Bonner is Ms. Garcia's lawyer. If Tobias had wanted one, I would have done it for him, dorko."

I hadn't thought of that little tidbit. She handles all of Toby's legal indiscretions. Why would this be any different? It makes sense that Amelia would want one. She sang her way up from the streets to get where she was. Obviously she'd want to protect herself.

"So are you saying you wouldn't need a pre-written document

to marry me?"

"Babe, the marriage isn't legal in the U.S., why would I want to bring technicalities into it? Besides, there is plenty of money to go around. I can part with money, I just couldn't part with you."

"Still want to go to Vegas for spring break?" I was excited again.

"Yes, but I want to wait and get married this summer in Holland." She was dancing.

"I will finish out the semester and take leave from work. The whole summer is ours. If I end up losing my job, I expect to be hired on as bartender at The Laine."

"I'll hire you as a waitress. I expect people to start at the bottom and work their way up."

"Was that a hint?" I asked while I reached for her bottom.

"Not now Doc. We have wedding plans to discuss. Tell me about your ceremony with Steven so we don't duplicate anything."

I really didn't want to discuss my first wedding. It was a part of me that I never felt comfortable talking about with her. "Not much to tell, we got drunk, decided to get married and six months later, I was Mrs. Steven Straightlaced."

"Hmm, cute last name, better than the real one. Where did you get married?"

"We got married at an Episcopal church in Houston. His family lived down there, and since my parents had to fly down anyway, we figured Houston would be easier for everyone. It was a small ceremony with fewer than a hundred people. My dad gave us ten thousand dollars which didn't even cover the cost of the reception. I got my dress at a sample sale for three hundred and my sandals came from a discount outlet for about four dollars and fifty cents."

"How did you pay for everything since you were both still students?"

"I had an old Mustang that I got in high school. It was in beautiful condition. You saw the pictures."

"Yeah, you said it was stolen." She looked puzzled.

"Well, in a way it was. I sold the car to a guy in Hillsboro for forty-eight hundred. Today it would be worth over twenty grand. Totally mint condition, low miles, perfect points and paint, fast and red." I sighed just remembering how much I loved that car.

"That's why you bought Mustang Sally last year?"

"Yeah, but Sally is nothing compared to the car I sold."

"So did you have a rehearsal dinner?"

"Oh yes. We took about thirty people to Bennigan's."

"Classy."

"Very classy. We had to wait three hours before they could seat all of us together. By the time we finally got a table, I was totally drunk. My bridesmaids and I were drinking flaming Dr. Peppers and Cuervo shots. I kept telling everyone that I didn't want to get married and they hushed me up really fast. Everyone said I just had cold feet. Eventually Jack and my maid of honor had to take me to the parking lot to quiet me down. I told them I couldn't marry Steven because I was in love with someone else. They asked me who I was in love with and I said 'anyone who doesn't have a dick'."

"You more or less said you were gay and they let you get married anyway?"

"I was hung over the next morning and just wanted to get it over with. Jack pulled me aside and asked if I was sure I was gay. I told him there was no doubt in my mind that I was meant to love women but I had to try to do the straight thing for the sake of our parents. He told me I was crazy and had a plan to get me out of there. I made him vow to keep his mouth shut. I was marrying my best friend and I would make the best of it and I did."

"Until the urge to kiss women got the best of you."

"No, until the suburban doldrums and constant resentment and fighting got the best of me. I did not kiss a woman until Steve and I separated. I am true to my word and I do not take vows lightly."

"Good to know."

"What about you? Think you can ignore the temptations of hot young women?"

"Doc, my eyes may wander but my heart, body and soul belong to you."

I sat down next to her on the floor and looked at a few old papers.

"So the wedding was a fiasco, how about the marriage itself? Were you completely miserable?" She adjusted herself to an Indian style position.

"It wasn't too bad at the beginning. Steven was my best friend and we did have a lot in common. We partied a lot and still managed to get our degrees. I think there was a certain stigma with my getting my doctorate the same day he got his bachelor's."

"A bachelor of what?"

"He was a business major with a minor in communications."

"So did he resent you?"

"Actually, I think I resented him a little. He got an amazing job right after graduation that paid twice what I made as a teacher. I lucked into the job at Central Woman's and devoted every waking second to moving my way up in the department. He hated living up there and I refused to move."

"You moved for me."

"I'd move mountains for you, Babe."

"But you did move to the suburbs with him, didn't you?"

"We did move near Dallas, but it was right before our separation. I was really only a suburbanite for six months or so." I lit another Marlboro.

"You have got to stop the casual smoking before you are hooked again. Give me a drag."

I handed her the cigarette and watched her choke on the first puff.

"So we were both working our asses off trying to reach our goals as fast as possible. We stopped seeing our friends, we stopped partying and before I knew it, we never saw each other except in bed."

"And how were things in bed?" She blushed a little.

"Aren't you the nosey one? Things were very awkward in bed, I used a lot of excuses. I didn't mind, um, doing things to him, but I hated when he tried to reciprocate."

She made an obscene gesture with her hand and mouth, I nodded and went on.

"I wouldn't have blamed him if he cheated on me or went to hookers, I probably would have preferred it so he'd leave me alone. He was nice about it and eventually he stopped trying completely."

"When did you know the marriage was over?"

"I reached a point where I missed my best friend and felt like I had no one to confide in. We started fighting about the stupidest things and I think I was just looking for an excuse to leave him. The more we fought, the more I thought about women. I even started sneaking peeks at his girly magazines."

"Mmmm, I can't see you reading porn." She made another obscene gesture and I kicked her.

"So one week he went on a business trip overseas and I was stuck at home recovering from knee surgery. I was doing online research for my novel and came across a link to a lesbian chat room."

"What were you researching that brought up a chat room on a search?"

"I don't remember, maybe I subconsciously typed it in. Anyway, I logged on to the site and before I knew it I was chatting with women around the world. I spent three solid days on the computer chatting with strangers and hiding my identity. I loved the fact that I could pretend to be anyone and no one would know the true me."

"So who did you pretend to be?"

"Actually, I pretended to be you—well, someone just like you. I was a wealthy, sexy young medical student. I was short with blue eyes and an athletic body. I actually started liking myself a little since in reality I was scraping by financially and I was forty pounds overweight."

"I still can't picture you fat."

"I like to think I was living in the pantry instead of the closet."

"So did you meet anyone good in the chat rooms?" She was intrigued.

"I did find someone in the chat rooms. As corny as it sounds, I found myself. I had thoughts and feelings that I hadn't had since I was an undergrad. I realized that I was a sexual being and that I was passionate and I discovered that I could feel more—" I got up for more coffee.

"Feel more what?" She handed me her cup.

"Just feel more. I wasn't a cold fish, I wasn't an angry person and I wasn't this fat professor who hated her body, her life and her future. When Steven returned, he came home to a new woman. I put myself on a diet, I started painting and writing again and I even started smiling. Three months later I was forty pounds lighter and Steve and I were friends again. We played pool every Friday and went cycling on the weekends."

"So the marriage was better? Why did it end?"

"The marriage wasn't better, the friendship was better. I realized that he was my best friend but that was as deep as it went. Once I accepted that, I decided to confide in him."

"So you told him you wanted out?"

"In a way. We were shooting pool and I made a remark about the waitress. He choked on his beer and laughed his ass off. He started asking me what type of woman I would be with if I was ever with a woman again."

"Again? He knew you had been with women?"

"We made our sex list, mine was quite extensive. Before we got married, I told him that I used to date women. He asked if it was going to be a problem, I assured him that I was done. Apparently

I wasn't. So anyway, we were shooting pool and talking about the ladies. I finally said, 'Steve, the thing is, I do want to sleep with women again. I am gay and I need to accept it.' He asked if I had met anyone and I told him I hadn't acted on my feelings. He was quiet for a few minutes and said, 'You need to go find her.' I asked him who I was supposed to find. He said I had to find the woman who would make me as happy as I made him. He said he loved me so much and with that love came the responsibility of making me happy. He said the only way he would ever make me happy would be to let me go to live the life I needed to live."

"Damn, he's a good guy." She seemed surprised.

"He is a good guy and I know he is happier now with a woman who adores him in every aspect."

"How is it that you never told me all this before?"

"You never asked."

For the first time in my life, I decided to be irresponsible and shirk work for the whole week. I called my secretary Tuesday morning and told her I didn't think I could make it back until the following Monday. I faxed some lesson plans and grade sheets to my TA. My secretary giggled every time I told her I was under the weather and every time I said "TA". Finally I asked what she found humorous about my poor health. She tittered and told me to have a good time at Toby and Amelia's wedding reception. Oh no—I had forgotten about it. Of course my secretary knew I would be attending, she was familiar with my living arrangements and had met the Laine family on several occasions. Also, the giggler received a phone invite from my partner when she called me in sick the day before. I tried to play it off and told her I hoped I would be well enough to attend the party. She told me to shut the hell up and go swimming. I took her advice and heated up the pool.

Unfortunately, I was flying solo for the week—not everyone can have the luxury of lying to their secretary. My partner tried to cut down her workload but feared it would make it impossible to leave over my spring break if she took this week off. I spent the latter half of Tuesday and most of Wednesday shopping. I was given a list and had a list of my own. We needed dresses, shoes, accessories and most importantly, a wedding gift. I had no idea what to get the newlyweds. What does one buy for people who can buy anything? I encountered this dilemma with her family every time Christmas rolled around.

I had no problem finding the perfect outfits for the reception. I preferred to do the clothes shopping for both of us. I felt I had a better idea of what looks good on her. If it were up to her, she would wear pajamas to work. Finding a gift was quite a conundrum. I searched malls, galleries, eclectic shops, even a feed store. I was tempted to get them matching cowboy hats, but dismissed the idea when I visualized a beauty like Amelia in a Stetson. I also hated to do the stereotypical "Dallas" thing. Just because of that darn TV show, people still thought we were a bunch of tycoons in ten-gallons. Of course, I was wearing a Shady Brady through NorthPark Center.

I finally gave up and fought the rush hour traffic home. Just as I walked in the door, I heard a voice on the answering machine. "Hey, I tried your cell. Where are you? Oh well. I thought of the perfect gift. I sent you an e-mail with an eBay link on it. The bidding ends in like twenty minutes. I am stuck in traffic. Can you be a dear and bid it? The sky's the limit, but try to do a last minute bid. That's always so much fun. See you soon. Bye Kitty! Bye Angel."

I hated it when people said *be a dear*. If I could be a deer I would shit in a forest and eat corn on a daily basis. I called her cell and got no answer, so I left a message that I would do the Ebay thing.

I logged onto my computer and found what she considered to be the perfect gift for Tobias. I was intrigued as to why it was so perfect. I was also torn between jealousy and panic. There was no way I could afford to chip in half. Bidding ended in thirteen minutes and it was already up to $17,000. Actually that seemed pretty good for a 1951 fully restored Ford truck. I was already in love with it. Bright, shiny red with white fenders. I quickly read all the details. The truck was warehoused in Houston for the past five years. It had relatively low miles and was definitely in mint condition. I had wanted a truck like that since I was in college. I saw an older couple driving one in a parade and had visions of a beautiful woman and myself loading flowers for our garden into the back. I wanted to cry, I was so truly jealous. With four minutes left, I put in a maximum bid of $22,000. Surely she would understand that the truck wasn't worth more than nineteen. I panicked at the last minute fearing that someone would have put in a bid for more. I hit refresh with forty seconds left and was still ahead. I relaxed a little. I hit refresh again and bidding had ended. In less than five minutes, I had managed to spend $18,375. It was exhilarating. I just had to figure out how to come up with an extra nine grand before Saturday.

"Hello, senorita!" A shout came from the kitchen. "Como estas? Did we get the truck?!"

"Hola! Yes, we won the truck. Pretty good deal too." I was hiding my jealousy.

"That's great. Hope you bid under my name so I can Paypal it easily."

"Yuppers. Tell me, fancy pants, why is that the perfect gift?"

She didn't hear me, she was struggling with her pantyhose in the closet. I followed her in. She was balanced on one foot and had the hose wrapped in five different directions. I caught her just as she started to tip over. She pulled herself back up and managed to free herself from the restrictive nylons. Next, she slowly unbuttoned her blouse and got my attention. I tugged on her skirt a little and she took the hint. She stood there before me, transforming herself from a determined lawyer into a dazzling goddess. I loved this transformation and tried to watch it every chance I got. I leaned in for a hug, her skin was warm and a little damp with rush hour sweat. I kissed her neck and moved up to her lips. She passionately returned the kiss and we made out in the closet for an hour. Finally she broke away and insisted on getting dressed for dinner, apparently she was famished. I was famished too but not for food.

"Let's go eat."

"First, tell me why the truck is the perfect gift for the newlyweds."

"I never said it was for Toby and Amelia. I just said it was the perfect gift."

We kissed for another hour before going out to dinner.

Chapter Fourteen

I was used to the extravagant parties of the Laine family. I was not used to the insane affairs of the Garcia entourage. We received a phone call two days before the reception from a man who asked a million questions. I was concerned that he was a member of the press and at first, I refused to answer his questions and passed the phone over to the Laine spokeswoman. When she got off the phone she told me it was a security check. I was surprised that he even asked what we would be wearing, even more surprised that she told him in such great detail. The guy probably got off.

We were supposed to be at the hotel at ten Saturday morning to spend time with Toby, Amelia and the families. We made the mistake of going to a friend's birthday party on Friday night and staying at a piano bar until after three. We forgot to set the alarm and neither of us woke up until after nine. We still had to pack our party clothes, dress for a day of brunching and schmoozing and pick up the gift at a gallery downtown. We ended up buying them a painting by a local artist.

The morning turned out to be a comedy of errors. I threw on a robe to run out and get the paper. I wanted to see the weather forecast. Silly me, the one time I didn't tie the belt on my robe, I was greeted by a few demanding members of the press. I took one step onto the porch and heard the clicking and whirring of dozens of cameras. I heard someone shout, "She's just the roommate," and they all stepped back to let me by. I asked if anyone knew the weather forecast and got three contradicting answers. I assumed they worked for three different papers. I locked the door behind me.

"Hey, roommate, there are a buttload of people on your porch. The good news is they got some great shots of my blowing robe and me in all my glory. The bad news is they will never print the photos because I am prosaic."

"You are not prosaic, sweetie." She blew me a kiss. "Now get in the shower with me and tell me what prosaic means."

I dropped my robe and hopped in the shower. She was humming the theme from "Close Encounters." I wasn't sure why she chose that particular piece but decided to hum along. I reached for the soap the same time she did and a brawl ensued. She pushed me at arms length and I threw fake punches. I tickled her ribs and she dropped the soap. Neither of us bent to pick it up just because of the obvious joke. We both kept saying "After you, no after you." Suddenly the shower door burst open and there was Tobias Q. Laine reaching for the soap.

"Geez, this could take all day, allow me to get it," he drawled and handed me the bar.

I put my embarrassment aside and pulled him into the shower. I wrapped my soaking body around his and pretended to hump his leg. His sister showed no sign of blushing and joined us in the embrace. Everything would have been fine if I didn't look through the foggy shower door and see a gorgeous stranger laughing her ass off. Oh my gawd, what a time to meet the sexiest celebrity on the planet.

"Hey Tobes, please tell me your parents aren't watching from the bedroom."

"Nah, it's just me and the ol' ball and chain." He winked at the sexy celebrity.

We finished sharing the soap and rinsing off. Amelia Garcia stood at the shower door passing out towels. For some reason I felt very comfortable with the scenario. I already felt a sort of family bond with her and my thoughts of her being a hottie ceased immediately. We gave Toby some dry clothes, adjourned to the kitchen and passed around the coffeepot.

"I guess introductions aren't necessary," Toby said.

"What's funny to me is that the way Tobias described you two, I thought you were both his sisters. I really had no idea that you were lovers until a few days ago."

"Partners," the rest of us said in unison. We all agreed on the idea that lovers last all night but partners are there forever.

"I'm sorry, partners." She blushed. Her accent was wonderful.

We spent twenty minutes hearing details of the Vegas wedding and told them of our own wedding plans. Toby was thrilled at the thought of summer in Amsterdam. Amelia promised to come along if it didn't interfere with her summer tour.

We had to come up with a game plan for the day. We were already an hour late for meeting the families at the hotel. We still had to pack and pick up the painting. The press population doubled since word got out that the couple was in the house. Toby decided that his sister and his wife should exchange clothes. Amelia and I would linger, pack and head out in an hour. The other two would take my Mustang from the garage and go get the art. It seemed like a logical plan, trying to fool the press but I knew they wouldn't give up so easily. We decided to give it a try. If it didn't work we would call Amelia's security guys to come get us out.

My girl looked great in Amelia's hip-hugger jeans, unbuttoned oxford and white jog bra. I was sorry to see her leave. I peered though the peephole and watched the Mustang pull down the drive and head down the street. Toby drove so fast that people had no chance to approach the car. One guy ran halfway down the block and came back in a pant saying, "It was her, let's go to the hotel." The plan worked and everyone cleared out except one small woman and her huge camera.

I finished dressing and packing and still had twenty minutes to kill. The determined photographer was still outside and a couple others joined her. I went to the den and found Amelia watching "SpongeBob SquarePants." My cat was batting at her hair and she didn't seem to care.

"Want some more coffee?" I offered.

"Any chance you could make it Irish? I don't normally drink before noon but I am on vacation and I am rid of agents, managers and fans for a few hours." She sounded apologetic.

I went to the bar and found a bottle of Bushmills. I poured us each a large cup of coffee and added the whiskey, some sugar and whipped cream. I only had enough for one round, which was good because I still had to drive us to the hotel.

"Thanks. I love your house. I expected something grossly extravagant based on the Laine reputation. This is quaint. I don't mean that in a bad way. It's a wonderful home."

"We fell in love with the area and the house. We thought about buying something newer but a 1930s bungalow seemed to suit our personalities." I was proud of the house and glad it was clean.

"What's it like?" she asked without elaborating.

"What? Being gay?" I was caught off guard.

"No, being normal, having a nice life without having to worry about the public eye."

"Well, I've never known it any other way. We have our moments in the spotlight because of the Laine family. Until I met them, I was just a run of the mill English teacher. Don't you remember what it was like before you got famous?"

"I went from living on the street to being on stage. I never had a middle of the road. I envy that. I hope one day Tobias and I can have some kids and just be normal."

"I hope so too. But I fear Toby will never be normal. I can tell he adores you though, maybe you can get him to slow down and be a family man."

"Here's to family." She held out her coffee mug and clinked it against mine.

I looked outside and saw only the one little lady.

"We are down to one photographer outside. She looks mighty determined. It's probably her big break." I dragged our suitcase to the kitchen and started preparing to leave.

"Just one, eh?" You could tell she had an idea. "What car are we taking to the hotel?"

"We can take the Boxter, the Jeep or my car."

"Think those might be a little obvious?" I knew where she was going with this.

I went outside and signaled the lady with the huge camera to come up on the porch.

"Morning! You're the last man standing, eh?"

"Yes, I am afraid so. I will leave though if you want me to."

"Actually, do you have a car?" I grinned.

"Yes, the red Honda," she pointed toward the street.

"Great, come inside." I pulled the door wide open.

Amelia came out from the den and the woman about fainted. She stood there frozen, her camera hand twitched and she resisted the urge.

"Hi! Great to meet you!" Amelia extended her hand and the lady shook it.

"Hi Miss Garcia, nice to meet you."

"Call me Amelia. Here's the deal. My sister-in-law and I are going to have a few shots of tequila. When we are through we want you to drive us to the Laine Hotel. If you promise to keep it to yourself and not take any pictures, we will let you bring your camera and one roll of film to the reception tonight."

I was thrilled that she referred to me as an in-law. The woman looked astonished and agreed to our terms. She thanked us profusely saying that she might actually make rent next month if that was okay with us that she sold the pictures. We told her to milk them for every penny and pay rent for a year.

The amazing, beautiful, Latina pop star and I sat in my quaint kitchen and did three shots of Cuervo. It was one of the best moments of my life. I only wished my lover-partner was there to share it.

Amelia and I arrived at the hotel giddy and in one piece. The red Honda lady pulled away with two crisp hundred dollar bills to buy some film and a dress. One more tequila shot and it would have been five hundred. We raced up twenty-two flights of stairs to the Honeymoon Suite. The elevator area was jam packed with conventioneers. I thought I was going to die after the climb and regretted the few cigarettes I smoked over the last week. The siblings were nowhere to be found. I called the front desk, they had no idea where the two might be. Next I called Toby's cell phone. I could barely hear him when he answered.

"Tobes! Where are you guys?" I shouted to be heard.

"We are at my belated bachelor party!" He shouted back.

I knew she would take him out. I made a guess that they were at Fred's, a strip club in west Dallas.

"Tobes! Where's the party?"

"At Fred's, silly. You know how we are! Come meet us!"

"I can't. I just got your wife drunk and now I don't want to take her out in public."

"Yeah, she's a pretty disgusting drunk," he teased.

"Put my girlfriend on!" I heard him pass the phone.

"Baby, do you have enough ones?" I knew she did.

"Sweetmeat, no one can beat your happy butt dance. I will save my ones for you." I heard Toby groan in the background.

"When are you coming over here?" I was anxious to get my dollars.

"We just got our check. I didn't want to leave the painting in the car in this neighborhood, so we still need to swing by the gallery. I will see you in an hour. Hasta."

My new friend was listening to her voice mail and looking a little irritated. Apparently her new parents-in-law were in the rooftop bar and wanted her to join them. They knew Toby would be off being wild. They thought this would be a great time to get to know her.

"They're not so bad," I told her. "You just have to keep the martinis flowing and try to avoid political discussions."

"Come with me," she pleaded.

"Not on your life. They scare the shit out of me." We laughed and the next thing I knew, we were headed to the roof.

Arthur and Anna were belly up to the bar playing video trivia. Interesting sight, to see a multimillionaire shouting out answers like, "Morris the cat!" and "Navel piercing!" We pulled up barstools next to theirs and helped with a round of answers. I was good at the literature questions, Amelia was great with American history—who knew? We shared a bottle of champagne and finished a few more rounds of trivia before the interrogation began. I felt so sorry for the bride.

"The papers say you don't have any family?" Anna started.

"Well, I would like to think I have family now." Amelia smiled at me. Good answer.

"No, I mean the Garcias. Where are your parents?"

"My mom died when I was ten and my dad was killed when I was eleven. I have been by my own ever since." Her English got worse the more nervous she became.

"How utterly awful. How ever did you survive?" Arthur interjected.

"I sang on corners and in mercados. I created a little street following that led me to meeting my manager." She seemed so young and shy all of the sudden, almost ashamed.

"Where did you live before coming here?"

"I grew up in Matamoros, Mexico and came to the U.S. when I was sixteen. I was very close to the Texas border, so I feel very at home back in Texas. I had my first singing job and little apartment on South Padre Island." She seemed confident again.

The third degree continued for another half hour, then they turned their attention to me.

"Well, you must be thrilled to have a new person to help you deal with the Laine headaches. Of course, she will legally be family. You can run off at any time." Anna sneered.

"I've put in a lot of years, legal or not, I think I will stick it out." I snapped back.

"Well, when you marry in Holland it will be as close to legal as you can get." Amelia added.

The in-laws looked at each other then pointed their glares at me. I did my best to remain calm and prepared myself for a painful afternoon.

"Did I speak out of turn?" The singer was batting her eyelashes. I think she knew exactly what she was doing. She was establishing sides from the get-go. She was very much on my side. God bless her, she had great intentions, just awful timing.

"I guess you hadn't heard. We only made the decision recently. We planned on telling you together when the plans were finalized. We only told Toby and Amelia this morning."

Arthur glanced at his watch and thanked the bartender. No tab to settle but he didn't tip either. What a putz. The grown-ups gathered their things and headed off to their room. Amelia and I stayed behind to have a beer and tip the bartender. Just as we started a game of trivia, the siblings came in.

"We ran into Mom and Dad on the elevator. They looked pissed. What happened?"

Amelia jumped first, "I opened my big mouth and told them

about your wedding plans."

"I told you she was a disgusting drunk," Toby laughed and kissed her.

"I think she is wonderful. I can't think of any other way I would have liked to have told them. Well, except for maybe having all involved parties present," I laughed and kissed my own girl.

The four of us sat and laughed and told stories for hours. I can't remember a better day. It was a shame we had to cut it short to get ready for the reception.

We took the last room remaining at the hotel so we could change clothes and shower. Room service brought up a cart full of appetizers, wine and roses. We changed into robes and lounged on the bed eating brie and crackers.

"Know what this reminds me of?" I wiggled my eyebrows.

"Out first date? You were such a slut?"

"Yup, our first date and you took advantage of me."

"Kinda makes me horny, know what I mean?" She winked cartoonlike.

"I know what you mean. Too bad we only have an hour."

She ripped off her robe, shoved the service cart aside and straddled me. I guess an hour was plenty of time. We made love and laughed. We talked and laughed. We were closer than ever lately. We were happy. We were late for the reception.

We rushed through much needed showers, fixed each other's hair and slapped on makeup. I have to admit, for doing it in such a hurry, the results were fabulous. We looked picture perfect; both in black formals (not matching, of course) and black stilettos. I loved black-tie events, especially when I was with the sexiest woman there. I was a little nervous when we got on the elevator. I hated lots of cameras but was reassured that the press was not allowed in the building. Just as the elevator slowed to the ballroom floor, my beauty in black leaned in and whispered.

"I asked Toby if we could have his sperm."

I hoped she was just trying to distract me from being nervous.

I held my equanimity and didn't miss a beat. "Well then, tell him we'll pick it up tonight."

The doors opened and a million people stared as we entered the hallway hand in hand. We spotted her parents greeting guests by the ballroom doors. Usually we drop each other's hands when we see them. This time we held on tight. Across from them were Tobias and Amelia Garcia-Laine. He looked adorable as always, and she looked like a vision in red. We exchanged modest hellos with his parents and greeted the newlyweds like we hadn't seen them in years. Just as I reached in to hug Amelia, the red Honda lady snapped our picture. One gone, thirty-five to go on the single roll of film. We attempted to pose for a few shots but she wasn't interested. She wanted candid moments. I made a mental note to behave until I saw her finish the roll.

The guest list, though impressive, was rather small. I expected at least five hundred people and was surprised to see fewer than two hundred. I met a fair share of politicians, rock stars, actors, authors, comedians and regular socialites. It was quite a guest list for such short notice. DFW airport must have been overrun with private jets over the past few days. I was most impressed with the band they hired for the affair. It was a simple local trio who played a few cover tunes, a few originals and not once did they attempt to trifle with an Amelia Garcia song. They alternated every half hour with the hotel's staff deejay. We all danced and drank, sang along and danced some more. Suddenly, my partner and I noticed a potential problem.

It seemed that the Vision in Red was about to dance herself out of her dress. Few people noticed, those that did were probably excited at the prospect. I looked around and saw the red Honda lady still waiting for the perfect shot. I pulled my girl aside so we could address the problem.

"Herb, we need clean up on aisle five," I mused.

"Nice dress, bad elasticity." She was serious.

We rambled and giggled back and forth for several minutes

about the situation. We didn't want to draw attention to her by saying anything and we didn't want her exposed on the front page of Sunday's paper. I finally came up with a solution. I asked the hotel manager to crank up the air conditioner to full blast. You could feel a definite chill in the air almost immediately. I swear I wasn't trying to make the outcome more alluring than before. Once we saw people commenting on the cold, we made our move. I borrowed a tuxedo jacket from a waiter, then subtly told Toby that a real gentleman would give his new wife his jacket. He followed directions like a good new spouse and all was well. Sunday's front page was a picture of the couple with a hotel mogul and mystery writer.

We partied until the wee hours of the morning and poured ourselves into bed as the sky outside grew lighter. I lay in the quiet hotel room for an hour and couldn't fall asleep. I didn't hear any snoring next to me.

"You still awake?" I whispered.

"No, I'm sleeping like the angel that I am."

"The angel that drank her weight in whiskey."

"Lying next to the angel that drank twice her weight in beer."

"Touché," I sighed.

I rolled onto my side and wrapped my arms around her.

"I can't sleep."

"No shit?"

"Can't you sleep either, Grumpy?"

"Not with you talking so much, Doc," she teased.

"Sounds like we are in bed with the Seven Dwarfs."

"One more whiskey and that might have happened."

"Yeah, what teen band was crawling all over you all night?" I was dying to know.

"I don't know. Three Blondes and an Ass. They're all the same."

I squeezed her tighter and wanted to crawl inside her soul.

"Baby?"

"Mmmmm."

"Did you really ask your brother for his sperm?"

"Yes." She was whispering.

"You want me to get pregnant?"

"Well, if *I* used Toby's sperm we'd have three-headed kids. Or one kid with three heads."

"We never even discussed this. I appreciate that you want to have your own genes involved, but shouldn't we have discussed it first? I thought we'd start out slowly with a few cats, maybe a dog, then work our way up to humans. You always said you wanted to be pregnant one day."

"You said you wanted to be pregnant too. I just figured because of the age difference that your clock would tick first." She tried to be casual.

"I have been hitting snooze for many years. I can hit it a few more. There are so many things I'd like to do before starting a family. Travel, work, explore life, sleep, you know, the basics."

"I have no problem with that. I don't know what compelled me to ask Toby. Forgive me?"

I squeezed her as tightly as I could and she squeaked.

I tried to sleep and it just wasn't going to happen. My mind was racing and I needed entertainment. I could tell by her breathing that she was still awake too.

"Sweetie? Why are you here?"

"Well, I got shitty drunk at my brother's wedding reception and I felt the need to lie down as soon as possible."

"No, jackass. I mean why are you here with me. Why did you pick me when you could have had any woman in the world. Why did you pursue me on the Internet and at Splinter's?"

She rolled over to face me and propped herself up on some pillows.

"I'd seen you playing pool for a long time. I watched you with Steven and I watched you with numerous different women. I always liked watching the way you interacted with people and one day I found myself critiquing the women you were with. It occurred to me that I was saying things like 'she's too good for that guy", then later, 'she's too good for that woman.' I realized that I was protective of you, a perfect stranger. I asked some people in the bar about you and they said that you were good people."

"So you went after me based on what other people said?" The thought seemed odd to me.

"No, I went after you based on the fact that you were the only person in the world that ever made my heart race. I had never even talked to you, yet I thought about you all the time."

"You were obsessed with an older stranger?"

"Obsessed is an ugly word. I prefer *fascinated*. Do you remember a night about a month before we met where we actually spoke?"

I racked my brain for a bit. "You'd think I would remember that but I don't."

"You were trying to put money in the jukebox, but it wouldn't take your wrinkled dollar. I walked over with a handful of quarters and asked you what you wanted to hear. You said, 'Dancing in the Moonlight by Toploader'. I dropped the quarters in and hit F-seven."

"Why don't I remember that?" I felt bad.

"Well, twenty minutes later you were stumbling toward home, drunk off your ass and the woman you were with left in a cab."

"Aha, I had alcohol blockage. I used to black out a lot."

"I know. Toby and I used to follow you home to make sure you were okay."

"How come you never told me that?" I was embarrassed.

"I didn't want you to think I was stalking you. Plus I didn't want you to be embarrassed about your drinking. You binged for a few months but you really slowed down after a while."

"So, knowing that I was a drunk who dated a bunch of losers, why did you still want to meet me?"

"You had a spark in your eye. You always looked hopeful and even when you were drunk, you were still nice to your dates. Not to mention the fact that you had a certain look about you that really gave me some spank fantasies."

"What look is that?"

"You have got to be the only college professor in the world who can make little round glasses look sexy. You can wear cowboy shirts with cargo shorts and look as good as you do when you are wearing high heels and garters. I used to lie in bed at night and wonder what you wore to work. I was tempted to audit one of your classes just to hear your voice."

"You're creeping me out, dude." I laughed so she knew I was kidding. "So did you have a profile on the Net? How did you meet women before you started stalking me?"

"You know all this, Doc. I heard from your friend, Jules, that you had a profile on that site."

"I know you have told me before, but I like the way you talk about the women you dated before me."

"Turns you on, does it?" She laughed and grabbed my breast.

"No, just makes me appreciate the fact that you chose me. What was the strangest date you ever had?" I was hoping she wouldn't say I was the strangest.

"I went on a date with a woman with huge knuckles who actually turned out to be a guy."

"No way!" I realized she was making fun of one of my past dates when I heard her laugh.

"No, seriously, I had my share of odd dates. I went to the gay bars to meet women or I would luck out and stumble across a lesbian at school or at the hotel. Keep in mind that I have been with you since I was twenty-two, I didn't have a lot of bar time even with my fake ID. I did meet a petite little flower on the elevator of the San Antonio hotel when I was nineteen. I was down there for a family reunion and I was going insane with all the old relatives telling me how cute I used to be. I decided to sneak off to my room to get stoned so I took the elevator up to Toby's and my room. On the ride up, the elevator stopped on the third floor and a short, young blonde got on. She was headed to the rooftop bar and we made some fast small talk. Before you knew it, we were both at the rooftop bar sipping Amstel Lights and sneaking hits off a joint."

"You smoked pot in front of the hotel staff? You bad little girl!" I was shocked.

"I knew they wouldn't tell daddy since it was the staff members who were selling it. Anyway, we bullshitted for about an hour—"

"Bullshat." I had to interrupt.

"We bullshat for about an hour and I realized that I had to get back downstairs before they came looking for me. I told the blonde that I had to go and she pulled me behind a fig tree and stuck her tongue down my throat. It was a totally awkward kiss and I literally gagged. I made up some crappy excuse about how I was caught off guard so she wasn't offended. We stared at each other for a minute then she said, 'Well, I gotta head out myself. We're having a family reunion in the main ballroom'."

"Holy shit! She was a relative?!" I was laughing my ass off.

"Can you imagine? I freaked out thinking I had just kissed my first cousin. I immediately asked her last name and she said *Laine*. I was practically in tears and ready to jump off the roof. I told her I was Arthur's daughter and she calmed me down by telling me that it was no big deal-that she was married to my cousin Jimmy. I was so relieved."

"Damn, I bet you started asking names after that." I was still giggling. "Tell me another bad date story."

"The sun is fixin' to come up." She yawned.

"So, we'll order breakfast and watch the sun rise." I reached for the phone and called room service.

She opened the curtains and hopped back on the bed. "I'll tell you about an awkward scenario if you promise not to get mad."

"I hate it when you tell me not to get mad." I felt the heat rise in my face.

"It's kinda funny, give my story a chance." She laid her head on my stomach.

I stroked her hair and she continued. "Remember that night we went to The Library for your poetry reading?"

I nodded.

"I was so freaking hung over the next day that I threw up at the office."

"I remember, you said what you do in the privacy of your office is your own business."

"Well, there was more to the story. I was in the washroom spewing my guts out when one of the partners came in. She asked if I was okay and I assured her that I was fine. She offered me a mint and a washcloth and I was grateful for both. We chatted for a bit and she asked if I had the flu. I was very evasive, not wanting to admit that I was seriously hung over. She took my being vague to mean that I was trying to cover up the fact that I had morning sickness."

"She thought you were pregnant? How funny!"

"She did. I considered playing along with the assumption but I realized that I didn't want a rumor spread around my office. I reminded her that I was gay and informed her that my vomit was induced by whiskey and not by sperm."

"Why would that story make me mad?"

"Well, I guess the fact that I am gay fascinated her. The next day she called me to her office, when I got there, she asked me to close the door. I expected a lecture on alcoholism among attorneys but instead I got a hand on my knee and an attempted kiss."

I stared at her waiting for the punch line.

"I didn't want to embarrass her by shoving her away, so I turned my head sideways and she kissed my ear. I managed to break away and as I walked toward the door I said, 'I am in a serious relationship with a woman who has herpes so I would be careful before you try that again'." She stared at me.

"Aha, so I'm not supposed to be mad about the kiss, I am supposed to be mad about the herpes rumor?"

"Yeah. Sorry about this, but when we go to this year's Christmas party, can you maybe sport a cold sore?"

"I will do my best."

We chatted all through breakfast as we watched the sun come up.

Chapter Fifteen

I shouldn't have played sick with only two weeks until spring break. When I returned to my office Monday morning, it was one nasty ordeal after another. As usual, there were overly dramatic students asking for extra credit or extensions on assignments. We had problems with text book approval, budgeting for renovations and on Sunday, a pipe burst in the department's main lecture hall. Gregor disappeared on Wednesday and no one had the guts to call me. We had to reroute classes to other buildings until the pipes were repaired and the rooms were cleaned. Water flooded my office and destroyed most of the books on my lower shelves including a first edition Dorothy Parker.

I decided to stay near the college Monday night to help with the cleaning and repair. I left a message at home that I would be staying at the College Inn. I laid books out all over tables hoping they would dry. I submerged myself in grading papers and filling out claims until I couldn't see straight. Around one in the morning, I made my way to the old dorms that were reconditioned into a flea bag motel. I had checked in earlier when I took a dinner break knowing that the lobby closed at eleven. All I could see before me was sleep. I had been up since before five and had been running all day. When I got to my room, the bathroom light was on. I didn't think anything of it or was too tired to care. I skipped my nightly face and teeth routine and immediately fell on the bed. I thought I was dreaming when I awoke to someone whispering my name—a rush of adrenaline made me bolt up. The voice was familiar but not familiar enough. The room was pitch dark.

"I have a gun," I said.

"No you don't. You're a pacifist." She giggled.

"I have a knife," I tried.

"No you don't. You're a klutz."

"I have a big dog." My last attempt.

"No you don't. You're allergic."

"You know too much, now I must kill you." I suspected who she was.

"Tobias tells me everything about his girls."

"Amelia?"

"Who did you expect? A serial killer?"

"A serial killer would have been less of a shock."

I flipped on the bedside light and saw the profile of a beautiful young celebrity. I threw my arms around her completely relieved that it wasn't a serial killer. She explained that she and Toby planned on staying in Dallas but Arthur sent Toby on an emergency trip to London for some "wild *coose* case." Amelia's "people"—body guards, manager, assistants—were on vacation for the rest of the month. She couldn't handle fighting off airport crowds by herself, so didn't go with Toby. She was already "too bored for words" so she went to our house and found out I was up at the college. She thought it would be fun to steal my old Mustang, drive north and surprise me. Boy, was I surprised.

We ordered a pizza and sat up talking for an hour or so. I was so tired but the fright gave me a second wind. She rambled on about married life, the search for a house, the problems with the Laine parents and her wish for anonymity. I rambled about the talk of having a baby, the thought of quitting the college and all the problems I had at work that day. She instantly became one of my best friends and it was so nice to get an unbiased point of view on things. She gave great advice and was very down to earth. I felt nostalgic—it was the glow I felt when my sister Amy and I sat up talking late. Part of me wanted to cry from thinking about my own twin in such a fond way. I missed her. The other part of me felt as though I had found a sister in Amelia. I hung on her every word and didn't even mind when she stole all the pillows and fell asleep while I was talking.

I woke up the next morning to a blaring TV and a sweaty Latina "trying to work off that late night pizza" with sit-ups. We decided that she should sneak out and head back to Dallas before anyone saw her. I gave her my house key and told her to stay with us until her husband returned from the "*coose* case." She was grateful and promised to do all the cooking. I already couldn't wait for dinner.

I made it through Tuesday's work completely caffeinated. I was at the coffeehouse so many times that the manager threw in a free T-shirt with my sixth mocha. I told him I would be back six more times in hopes I could get the matching ball cap. I made it back only once more before my blood pressure told me I should switch to water. I didn't actually drink the water, I splashed it on my face and tried to freeze my eyeballs open. I caught up on work, managed to coherently teach all my classes and mopped the entire first floor. Around seven o'clock, my secretary found me sleeping in a ball underneath my desk. She offered to make me a hotel reservation but I remembered Amelia's promise to cook. The image of her in an apron was enough to keep me awake on the drive back to Dallas.

When I pulled onto our street I saw tons of cars. I was surprised, however, when I didn't see any news people in front of our house. I barely squeezed between two Hummers to pull into the empty driveway. I gathered my briefcase, grabbed the mail and heard music coming from the house. When I walked in the front door, I was greeted by a familiar face. I couldn't place the name but remembered the woman from an Indie film we saw at the Magnolia the month before.

"You must be the elusive professor." She took my briefcase and handed me half a warm beer.

The adjective *elusive* bothered me a little so I nodded and smiled. I scanned the room and saw an interesting mix of our friends and minor celebrities. Everyone was glowing and talking wildly. No one even noticed my presence. I made my way to the kitchen and found Amelia dancing with my girl. My heart sank and the term elusive haunted me again. I tiptoed to the refrigerator and found a cold Corona then I seated myself on the kitchen counter awaiting discovery.

"Doc!" My girl stopped dancing and blushed, "You're home!"

"A day late and a dollar short but I'm here."

"Everyone, this is my fiancé." She was drunk, she would never call me that around strangers.

I smiled as best I could and raised up my beer. Amelia continued dancing to the beat of her own music.

"What's going on here? Is the IFC filming in our living room?" I shouted over the music.

"No, we were making *sinner* and thought it would be more fun to cook for forty than for two."

"Three." I corrected. "You were making *sinner* for three, right?"

"Right, cooking for three." She looked confused.

"What time did you get home from work." I wondered how she could be so tanked by nine.

"I took a half day off to help Amelia move some stuff over. She's gonna stay for a few weeks."

"I thought we were going to Vegas next week." I was obviously annoyed.

"Oh, yeah. We were thinking that Vegas could wait until the summer." WE? WE were thinking. The pronoun echoed in my head and I wished I'd stayed at the flea bag another night.

"I thought we were going to Holland this summer. Are WE postponing that until Christmas?"

"No baby," she took my hand, "Holland is still a go. We can do both."

Amelia finally came back to earth and noticed my presence.

"Roomie!" She kissed me on the cheek. "Isn't this fun?"

"It's great," I lied, "Too bad Toby is missing all the fun."

"He sends his love, he has to stay a few weeks in London. Problems at the hotels there, a strike or something."

I wondered what happened to the "*coose case.*" I silently questioned how anyone could predict how long a strike would last. I prayed that it was a legitimate problem and that Toby wasn't making pretext to go on a London bender sans spouse. My partner winked at me and crossed her fingers. I realized then why we needed to house the superstar and postpone our trip. The last thing we wanted was for her to get lonely and hop on a plane to England only to find her new husband in bed with a blonde Brit. I loosened up a little and had some cold spaghetti and another beer.

The group of misfits started to clear out around midnight. We had a good time playing "I Never." I learned some interesting facts about B movie people, swearing that I would never speak of the tidbits to anyone. Amelia passed out on the sofa shortly after the last guest left. We wrapped her in a blanket, kissed her on the forehead and headed to bed ourselves.

"We can't distract her with a party every night you know." I said while washing my face.

"I know, but at least we are both off work next week. Maybe we can find something to entertain her. I'm sorry about the Vegas thing. I wasn't able to confirm the hotel strike, so I didn't want to take any chances."

"I understand, baby. I just got a little worried. She is young, beautiful, famous, fun and apparently open to anything." I whispered in case our guest was up and wandering the halls.

"She is all that, but you have two things she doesn't have."

"What might those be?" I expected to hear big boobs and large hands.

"The two things she doesn't have?"

"Yes ma'am."

"My heart and my soul."

"Great answer!" My heart jumped.

"I know!" She stripped her way to the bedroom. I stripped right behind her.

The three of us behaved the rest of the week. We rented movies, ate junk food and confirmed that there was indeed a strike at London's Laine Hotels. Good Tobias, good boy. My new roommate spent Thursday morning autographing photos. On Friday, I rewarded my A students with the coveted treasures. I was coerced into giving the photos to my B, C, D and even my F students. I never let it slip that the woman they adored was sleeping in my guest room. I was bursting at the seams so I whispered the secret to my secretary. She swore she would not tell a soul. It only cost me five photos, a mocha and a bagel.

I finally got caught up on my work by staying late and coming in early. My drive home Friday evening seemed to take forever. I had nine days of fun and rest ahead of me. I couldn't get my little car to go fast enough. The cop who pulled me over felt that my car was going plenty fast. He let me off the hook when I gave him an Amelia photo. Those things worked better than cash. I promised myself I would use them for good and not for evil, then I made a mental note to ask her for twenty more.

I walked in the door of our beautiful bungalow and was greeted by two beautiful women wearing cowboy hats. One handed me a tequila shot and the other handed me some aspirin.

"What's this for?" I held up the aspirin.

"Drink the worm and trust us."

I let the insect slide down my throat then took the aspirin with some water. Amelia handed me a cowboy hat and another shot.

"Hey ladies, we have nine days, let's take it slowly." I took the shot anyway.

"Baby, I got some good news and some bad news." My girl handed me another shot.

"I'll take the good news today and the bad news a week from Sunday."

She handed me a set of keys and pointed toward the garage. I set down the tequila and jumped into her arms. She almost dropped me but carried me to the garage. That red truck looked better in person than it did on Ebay. I cracked the garage door and started the engine-it purred. I opened the door the rest of the way and the three of us piled in. The three of us drove around the neighborhood for an hour. We would have driven longer but Amelia feared she would *loose her buzz*. We went home and immediately gave her a beer.

"We are thinking about going out tonight. Amelia's manager might be able to get Sammy's bar to let us in the back door and close off an area for a few hours."

"Do you think that's safe?" I didn't want the secret to get out or she'd have to leave.

Amelia promised it would be okay. She assured me that people tended to leave her alone in bars. She figured they preferred to keep her there and have a story to tell rather than scare her off and have nothing. I told them I was in as long as none of us had to drive and as long as we had enough friends there to be deterrents.

She told me that they already invited twenty friends and three security guards. The hotel was sending the limo. I headed off to change clothes then remembered that there was bad news to go with the good.

"The truck is amazing, baby. Thank you so much. You made my day. What's the bad news?"

The two of them looked at each other and both handed me a beer. I took the fuller glass and slammed it, waiting for something awful.

"I won't candy coat it. I will tell you flat out. You may be upset at first but it might turn out to be a good thing. Just remain calm. We are here for you, don't worry about a thing."

"Geezus. Just tell me already!" I started to panic.

"Your mom called. They will be in Dallas for two days on their way to Spain."

I didn't know how to react. I don't think I remembered that I had just come out to my mom. What shocked me even more is that my parents were going to Spain. They never traveled.

"My parents are going to Spain?"

"Doc, I think you missed the point. They will be here overnight. You will have to entertain them."

"Well, hopefully I can stay at work late."

"They are coming on Tuesday. This Tuesday. There's more. Your mom said she didn't tell your dad that you are gay. She said you will have to tell him yourself."

"You talked to my mom?"

"No, she left all this on the answering machine. I saw the caller ID and steered clear."

I stared at my shoes, trying to think of a solution. I really wished we hadn't canceled our Vegas trip. I set down my beer glass and sat on the floor.

"Are you okay?" Amelia was genuinely concerned and sat down next to me.

I looked over at her big brown eyes. She had conquered so

much in her life. She had no family and didn't understand my plight. I grabbed both their hands and squeezed.

"I'm fine." I took a deep breath and faked a smile.

The three of us raided the closets and dressed each other. It was a little weird having someone else there but my partner and I didn't hide our affection or our bodies. Amelia didn't hide hers either which, honestly, thrilled me internally. Sammy's bar was pretty much a dive in downtown Dallas. We loved it because of its cheesy cover bands and cheesier nachos. We were all appropriately dressed in jeans, boots and the same old hats. When the limo arrived, we had the driver take some pictures of us while we finished our beers. He was more than happy to do it. I had to stop him on the way out and ask him to remove the film from his pocket. He apologized profusely and I gave him an autographed photo.

There are very few details to describe from the evening on the town. We got settled in at the bar. The band spotted Amelia and decided to play several of her songs—I should say butcher her songs. She was insulted. The crowd kept shouting and sending drinks. We got drunk fast and decided we should leave before Amelia took the stage herself. The highlight of the evening was this kid we met in the alley on our way out. When I say kid, I mean this twenty-something girl who looked as if the world hated her.

"Hey! I know you!" She started to head our way. Security hurried Amelia into the car.

The stranger continued walking our way and I caught a glimpse of her face.

"I know you." She said and pointed at me.

I recognized her as one of my students who disappeared mid-semester.

"Olympia?"

"You remembered!"

I approached her and noticed scars, dirt and pain on her face. I spent ten minutes talking with her to the dismay of the security guards. She brought me up to date on her abusive husband, miscarriage and loss of job. I gave her my card and told her to call, vowing I would find her some work and a place to stay. She was tentative yet grateful. All I could think about was how good I had it with all the love in my life and committed myself to making my parents' visit amicable.

Chapter Sixteen

Saturday morning, Amelia announced that she was going to be a good daughter-in-law and visit with the Laine parents for the day and night. We told her not to have too much fun and made her promise to return Sunday afternoon. She said she would be back as soon as possible and climbed into the Laine limo hung over and very irritated with the situation. As much as we hated to see her leave, we were secretly delighted to have a day alone together.

"Nap?"

"Okay, one hour, then we run errands and clean for your parents' visit."

"Argh." I poured out my coffee and threw away the cold pastries.

By the time I crawled back into bed, my mate had already set the alarm and was half asleep.

"Set it for an hour?"

"Mmmhmmm." She was out.

I lay there for about half an hour worrying about how I was going to tell my dad about my lifestyle. I knew he would still love me but I wasn't sure if he would ever speak to me again. My mom never did call me back after my big phone outing. I wondered if it would be better to put them in a hotel. The Laine hotel? No, too awkward. I decided that having them stay with us was probably the best idea, although I hated to overwhelm them with everything at once. At least Amelia would be here as a bit of a buffer. My mate rolled onto her back and let out a soft moan. She made a nap seem so sweet. I finally drifted off just as the alarm screamed its beep, beep, beep. In one dramatic motion, my girl jerked her entire body and bolted upright, unsure of what day it was. Unfortunately, during the body jerk, her elbow met my eye. I bolted upright as well, screaming out in pain.

"Ow! My funny bone!" she snapped still unaware of what was going on.

"Funny bone? My eye!"

"No really, I hit my elbow on something."

"I realize that. I am stating that the something is my eye!"

She let out a roar of laughter while rubbing her tingly elbow. I sat there with my hand over my left eye expecting blood to drip down. No blood, just a severe throbbing.

"It's not funny. That hurt like a bitch."

"I'm sorry baby. It was completely unintentional."

"How do I know that for sure? Maybe you subconsciously did it with malicious intent. Maybe you planned it for weeks. Maybe I should sue for damages."

"There you go! Let me call your lawyer for you. Hello, yes, this is she." She answered a pretend phone and shot me a devilish grin.

"Ha ha. I can find another lawyer, you know?" I sniffed.

"Yes, but I come cheap."

"And you come fast too," I crawled on top of her and kissed her neck. When I leaned over I was sure my head was going to explode. It was worth the pain.

We played and giggled for another hour before it occurred to her that ice might be a good idea for my eye.

"I'm fine, I don't need ice."

"Umm. Sweetie? I think you need a lot of ice, maybe an aspirin and definitely a mirror."

"Why? What's wrong?" I started to get up and felt dizzy.

She brought me a little mirror and there it was in all its glory-a black eye.

"Ice! Hurry! Shit . . . what will my parents think?" I started shouting. "Mom, Dad, this is my girlfriend, Mike Tyson. Mike, my parents."

She returned from the kitchen laughing hysterically with a bag of ice and a Shiner Bock.

"I don't see the humor in that." I smiled.

"You probably can't see much of anything. A Shiner for the shiner." She handed me the goods. After a while, the pain eased but the bruise got darker and darker. I always had awful timing.

We made it through the grocery store with few stares. I wore my reading glasses for subtle cover thinking that sunglasses would have been too obvious. I picked out things I knew my parents would like—sushi, granola, Nehi, pistachios, caesar salad, steaks, yams, the usual odd combination. They would only be at the house one night but I felt the need to buy enough food to last them a week. I knew it wouldn't go wasted with Amelia's friends dropping in at all hours. After we put the groceries away, we took a vote on what to do next. It was a landslide—we should postpone the house cleaning and go sit on a patio somewhere to lick our wounds. We called some friends and told them to meet us downtown at three for a "pre-coming out" powwow.

"Something in the shade, babe. I don't want to be bruised *and* burned."

"Geesh, you are starting to sound like a wife. Bitch, bitch, bitch."

We found a table with an umbrella close to the beer garden's bar. Our friends strolled in one at a time, each with a witty and unconcerned comment about my eye. It's a good sign that no one was worried, they knew the caliber of our relationship. We ordered a pitcher of margaritas and no one batted an eye when we stuck two straws in it and giggled like crazy.

"Okay, we have called you all here today for a reason." My lawyer sounded so professional. "Doc's parents are coming to stay with us Tuesday night. She has not yet come out to her father but her mom knows. To make matters worse, she ran her eye into my elbow this morning—in bed no less. Now we not only need a good coming out idea, we need a good black eye story."

"I know a good black guy story," our obnoxious friend Sarah interjected.

"Black *EYE*, you jackass. We all have a good black *GUY* story." Marianne snapped.

Our friend, Jules, stared at me for a few minutes as if to sum up the situation.

"Whatcha got, Jules? Why so pensive?" I pried hoping she had the answers.

"You are over thirty. You are a college professor, you have slept with this woman for a zillion years"—she pointed at my beauty—"and you have never told your father you are gay?"

"Yup. Does that make me a bad lesbian? Should I send back my erotica and flannels?"

"No, it makes you a coward. Are you ashamed of your life or of your partner?"

I started to get a little annoyed with Jules. "I'm very proud of both," I said louder than necessary.

"Then make it a fact, not a question. Do not wait for a response. It should be as definite as saying that the sun will rise tomorrow, it can't be argued, it can't be changed."

She made a good point and I appreciated that. It does seem like most people announce that they are gay then wait for a response. I don't need a response, I need him to know all that I am. I need him to know what makes me happy, who makes me happy; who inspires me, who I inspire. I need him to know that I am happy and that I am free.

"Thanks, Jules. Got any ideas for the eye explanation?" I asked as I lit a cigarette.

She grabbed an ashtray and hurled it at me.

"Um, thanks?" I caught it just before it hit my shoulder.

"Just think if you hadn't caught it, it might have hit you in the eye!" She smiled.

"That would work, but then I'd have to tell my parents that I smoke too."

"You're hopeless." Jules winked and stole a cigarette.

We got home relatively early Saturday night. Of course when you start drinking at three, you pretty much have to pass out by eleven. We got up early Sunday to clean the house. My eye wasn't any worse but it wasn't any better either. The chores were divided with the knowledge that if we worked in the same room we would get nothing done. I started in the kitchen and she chose to work on the pool, testing the chemical levels and skimming leaves off the top and bottom. After half an hour of scrubbing the kitchen counters, I glanced out the back window and didn't see my pool girl. I visually scoured the yard, the sides of the pool and the pump area; no pool girl. I checked the garage thinking she was getting hoses—no pool girl. I returned to my chores and thought I heard something on the roof. I stood quiet and heard nothing. I resumed cleaning and heard definite pounding across the roof. I ran to the back door and just as I slid it open, I saw a naked woman flying off the roof into the deep end of the pool.

I laughed my ass off and ran to the edge of the pool.

"Are you okay?"

"I'm fine. I was having problems cleaning." She spit water at me.

"You should try Windex."

"Windex?"

"Obviously your cleaning problems are caused by streaking."

She pulled me into the pool and held me under until I kicked her in the shin. We both swam to the top, giggling and playing.

"We should get back to work. Tuesday is around the corner and this house is far from spotless."

My naked beauty swam to the deep end in all her glory as I climbed out of the pool

"Ah, screw it. I got a maid service coming in the morning. Oh, and a pool man, a gardener, a decorator and a chef."

It never failed to astound me how simple life could be when you have money.

"Well then, what does that leave us to do?" I asked, feeling a little unnecessary.

"I dunno, a day of beauty?" she offered, knowing I would shun the idea.

"Mmmmm! You mean like manicures, waxings, haircuts, facials and shoe shopping!"

"Yes ma'am!" She was cringing already, awaiting my response.

"Okay," I was surprised I said yes. I hated being poked by strangers.

"Really?" She was amazed. "You would enter the Red Door?"

"I figure it couldn't hurt. Getting all femmed out and gussied up might help the big confession."

"Are you worried that they might think of us as stereotypical lesbians if we don't have our best, waxed faces on? You do realize that neither on of us even remotely appears gay. Well, except for your cowboy shirts and sandals." She swam toward the edge of the pool. I held up a towel for her and worried that the neighbor would peek over the fence again.

"Don't knock my cowboy shirts. I grew up on a ranch in the wild and wooly West. I am justified in dressing to suit my heritage."

"Oh, and the sandals? Did Annie Oakley wear those in the off season?" she teased.

I pulled the towel away from her and headed back toward the house. As I walked in the door I shouted over my shoulder, "Hello Mrs. Jacobs! How's the garden?!" Then I locked the door behind me and looked out the window. The teaser obviously thought I was kidding and called my bluff by standing in full glory right in the middle of the patio. She dropped to the ground and crawled toward the door when she heard Mrs. Jacobs reply, "Hello dears. The garden is great, thank you."

"Hellloooo! Let me in!" she begged.

"No. Not until you apologize for making fun of me." I tried to hold back a laugh, but she looked so desperate all hunched over and hiding her goodies.

"Psssst. Lady, let me in and I will buy you some Lucchese boots and two new cowboy shirts."

"Why? What's wrong with my sandals?" I was laughing, watching her wave at the neighbor.

"Nothing. I am sorry I made the Annie Oakley remark. Let me in and I'll be your best friend."

I couldn't argue with that. I opened the door and she crawled in on all fours. I scratched her behind the neck and offered her a treat.

We took a little time to water all the plants and sort through the dry cleaning that had been sitting in its plastic for over a week. I took a shower while Miss Fancy Pants called to make us a spa appointment.

"Bad news. The spa doors at NorthPark remain locked on Sundays." She looked so dejected.

"What about one of the other places or the hotel salon?"

"No one is open on Sundays. Well, no place decent anyway.

I'd be more than happy to treat you to a barber shop and the nail salon at the mall."

"Hmm, that's tempting but I fear I might leave there with a mullet and nine toes."

"Hey, isn't Amelia coming back here this afternoon? I bet someone would open up for her."

"Are you telling me that you would use your superstar sister-in-law's name for your own personal gain?" I was surprised I didn't think of it first.

"If it means I don't have to have bad hair and thick eyebrows when I meet your parents, then yes, I will use her celebrity status."

We called Amelia and explained our dilemma. She was delighted to help us out and thrilled to have a spa day with the girls. She called back ten minutes later and said to meet her at Bottman's at two. Bottman's was the most upscale spa in the city, even the Laines had a hard time getting appointments there. We dressed in casual chic and got to the spa right at two. Amelia was already inside with a glass of champagne and a plate of fresh fruit in front of her. I was a little nervous about being pampered—I always thought the definition of that word was having diapers put on. A full staff of people were more than happy to give up a Sunday to meet their favorite pop star. We all decided to have our eyebrows waxed, our nails done and our hair cut. We took off in three different directions to let the games begin. I worried that they might not have enough champagne to get me through the day.

I sat rigid in the soft leather barber's chair and waited for my stylist. A blonde woman who smelled of pineapples and menthol cigarettes came in to help me pick my nail color. I opted for a French manicure since I refused to ever wear pink or red polish. Twenty minutes later, my hairdresser came in—I should say sashayed in.

"I am Lebron and I will make you wonderful. Lynette will make your nails perfect and Lenora will take care of your mustachio and caterpillar eyes." His thick accent was almost irritating.

"I am already wonderful. The mustachio will remain untouched." My upper lip had never been waxed and I wasn't going to start. I feared it would grow back thick and dark and I'd look like Frida Kahlo, although I didn't mind having the eyebrows done, I didn't want Frida's brows either.

"Oh, a woman who knows what she wants. Me like, me like." Lebron tittered.

Before I knew what hit me, Lenora had done her job. With very little pain, my eyebrows were perfectly shaped and my Brook Shields appearance was gone forever. Lynette started on the nails after Lebron's assistant shampooed my hair. It did feel really nice to get so much attention, especially attention to things I had neglected for so long.

"I am going to darken all of your hair then give you highlights. I will then trim off two inches to give you more body, then I will thin the front for a messy look." Lebron knew what he wanted.

"Um, do I have any say in the matter? How about just a trim?" I hoped I didn't piss him off.

"You want a trim, go to a barber. You come to Lebron, you get a whole new you."

I finished off my glass of champagne and braced myself for a long afternoon. The man was an artist who obviously loved what he was doing. He took extra time making sure that my hair perfectly framed my face. He was tedious with the highlights so that they weren't too thick or too slabby. The whole time he rambled about his wife back in Germany who left him for a rock star. The way he described the situation, you would have thought he was talking about John and Yoko. I asked him what kind of German name was Lebron. He told me that no socialite would trust her hair to a straight man named Adolf, so he became Lebron forty hours a week. I had to agree with the assumption.

Long after Lynette finished my nails and I had finished three glasses of champagne, the hair artist was finally done. I hardly recognized myself in the mirror. I had gone from conservative college professor to unkempt wild child. He blew my hair dry and didn't even comb it, it looked messy and low maintenance, and flat out amazing. I looked ten years younger and hadn't felt that good since the first night I played pool at Splinter's with what's her name. I practically kissed Lebron and thought he would have liked it.

I went to the lobby and found my two playmates already there waiting there for me. Amelia didn't look different at all, just a little shinier. I guess it is hard to improve upon perfection. My mate's hair looked a bit shorter from the back but nothing too drastic. When she turned around and looked at me, she appeared flat out shocked. Her mouth said nothing, but her eyes held a position of surprise.

"What?" I asked getting nervous. Amelia burst out laughing.

"What is it, don't look so shocked, I don't look half bad." I poked for a compliment.

My mate stood there, still in a state of awe then started bawling her heart out. I panicked and ran to her side. Amelia started laughing even harder and was practically on the floor. I wasn't amused.

"Baby, what's wrong? Why are you crying, why are you looking at me like that?"

Through sobs she replied, "It's my eyebrows. They waxed them funny and now I look like I am in a state of surprise even when I am not lifting my eyebrows!"

I held back a laugh and tried to comfort her. It didn't work. I took one look at her face and caught Amelia out of the corner of my eye. I lost it, flat out laughed. The surprised woman before me cried even harder. I offered a hug and she pushed me away.

"What happened?" I looked at Amelia and fought a smile.

Amelia calmed herself down long enough to respond. "Well, apparently your little lawyer friend here defended Lenora's brother-in-law a few months ago and the outcome was not positive."

"Okay, that makes sense. Is there any chance we can get them fixed?" I had to grin.

"No, they are too thin, I will have no eyebrows if we do any more waxing. How is this going to look in court if every time I question someone I look surprised by their answer?" She started to see the humor in the situation, thank God.

The salon owner came out to see what the problem was. Amelia immediately told him the situation and he was very apologetic. He offered to fire the evil Lenora but we told him it wasn't necessary. He was obviously concerned with his reputation when word got out at what happened to Amelia's sister-in-law. Our lawyer went through some tough negotiations and struck up a deal. Amelia would not tell the press and Lebron would personally come to our house once a month to cut our hair at the owner's expense. It sounded good to me.

As the three of us drove back to the house, I broke the silence with uncontrollable laughter. The timing was awful and I shared my thoughts, "Now what's gonna happen? Dad, I'm gay. He will look at you and think, wow, this must be big news, even her roommate looks surprised." We all laughed till we cried.

Chapter Seventeen

The doorbell rang Monday morning promptly at eight. Amelia let in the crowd of people who had arrived to make our house perfect. I was in the pool swimming laps when a kid the size of Andre the Giant stepped outside. I practically choked when I saw his size fifteen shoes and wondered if it was true about a man's shoe size. If so, straight women surely had their work cut out for them.

"Are you our pool genius?" I asked the obvious, he was carrying hoses.

"Yes ma'am." His voice was surprisingly squeaky.

I climbed out of the pool and dried myself off. I couldn't help but notice that he was staring. He'd probably never seen a woman over thirty so scantily dressed. I put on my robe and he never took his eyes off me.

"It's not polite to stare," I said, although I was flattered.

"You have a navel ring." he stammered.

"Yes, and a tattoo as well. I am branded for life." I was disappointed that he wasn't admiring my great haircut or my girlish figure.

"I'm sorry. It's just when I sat in your British lit class, I never would have guessed that you . . . well, that you had . . ." His voice trailed off.

I sat there perplexed for a minute. I taught at a women's college and although they did enroll men, I didn't remember having any who weren't petite and gay. I looked back at the student and it struck me, Andre the Giant was actually Andrea the Giant. I felt terrible and backtracked over our conversation to make sure I hadn't used any gender specific pronouns. I stared for a minute not knowing what to say.

"Well, you can't judge a book by its cover." I hope she caught the lit reference.

"Ain't that the truth," she blushed. "I thought you were bourgeois and you probably thought I was a guy."

I had no idea how to react although I was impressed that anyone could use the words *ain't* and *bourgeois* in the same sentence. I blushed and whispered, "Touché."

By ten o'clock, the house was in complete chaos. I didn't realize how much work it was having other people do your work for you. I helped the chef come up with a suitable menu. We opted for a Thanksgiving dinner. Whenever I imagined coming out to my parents, it was always during Thanksgiving dinner. I often pretended that it would be as easy as turning to my father and saying, "I like gams, pass the yams." I knew it would never be like that but the fantasy made me smile.

I told the gardener what flowers I preferred and begged him not to butcher my honeysuckle bushes no matter how much they littered the pool. I helped the pool girl get out of a never-ending conversation with the neighbor when she made the mistake of waving at her over the fence. I showed the cleaning crew where we kept all the clean sheets and tried not to be embarrassed when they found out that we did not own a toilet brush. I sat down with the decorator and told her what direction we were trying to go with the house. She couldn't grasp the idea of country-deco-mission-funk. We compromised on bright colors and as few flower patterns as possible. I went to the grocery store again and again until I finally got the right type of flour and the perfect toilet brush.

The house smelled of baked pies and Murphy's Oil Soap. It was starting to feel like home. I didn't realize how far we still were from actually being settled in. It looked as though the house would finally be perfect by the end of the day. If it went smoothly with my parents, my life would be perfect as well. I discovered that I was subconsciously crossing my fingers all morning. I wondered when that little habit began. It suddenly occurred to me that I was the only resident present. My roommates were no where to be found. I thought they might be hiding from all the pandemonium and called both their cell phones but got no answer. I gave up and went back to coordinating delivery men who were bringing in our monstrosity of a leather sofa and some accent tables. I was thrilled to see that the decorator stuck with sharp lines and dark wood.

By four o'clock, things had started wrapping up. The house was more or less furnished and even a few of the smaller walls were painted. The pool was crystal clear, the lawn was manicured and the bushes were tidy but not butchered. The counter tops gleamed and the toilet bowls sparkled. I was awed by the power of a good toilet brush. The chef had baked four pies and started on some side dishes. He would return on Tuesday to do the major cooking. Everything was breathtaking. Still, my roommates were no where to be found. I spent the next hour organizing the pantry and unloading the dishwasher.

"Hello? Is this our house?" The call came from the front door.

"Yes, welcome to 'Better Homes and Gardens'."

"My, my, doesn't it look wonderful in here!" Amelia shouted.

"Where were you guys all day?" I was secretly glad they were gone.

"We went shopping, we decided to get out of your way, sorry we forgot to call, babe." She gave me a kiss on my cheek.

"No problem, I had fun being the queen of the castle today. When did you sneak away?"

"We left after the pool guy got here." Amelia was dumping bags on my new sofa.

"That was not a guy. That was an ex-student, and a *GIRL*!" I grinned.

My partner did a double take, "NO way! That was a girl?"

I couldn't help myself. "Yes, our pool guy is a pool girl. Don't look so surprised!"

Amelia fell over laughing and I stood there, silently waiting for a response. She didn't say anything but I knew she'd get me back later.

We decided we shouldn't mess up the kitchen by cooking, so we ordered take-out ribs and had a carpet picnic on our new art deco throw rug. It took everything in our power not to touch the fresh baked pies. We debated for an hour and decided that it was important to sample the chef's recipe so we dug into a cherry pie—it was good but not the best I've had. I reminded myself that not everyone can use hand-picked cherries from a tree in their own backyard. The thought of that set me off into childhood nostalgia. I spent two hours briefing the other women about my parents, things that had happened in my youth and what I was afraid would happen after Tuesday's announcement.

They assured me that everything would be okay. Amelia said that no matter the outcome, she would still be my *sister*. I felt a little better knowing that I would always have a family. We finished off the entire pie and two pints of vanilla ice cream and headed for bed. I knew I wouldn't be able to sleep between the anxiety and sugar rush. My partner was pretty wired too, so we lay in bed channel surfing and chatting.

"Tomorrow's the big day, huh?"

"Yup." I was trying to get it out of my mind.

"Are you gonna invite them to our wedding?"

"Honestly, I hadn't thought about our wedding." I felt bad for admitting that it wasn't a priority.

"Gee, you know how to make a girl feel special." She switched channels.

"I was watching that." I wasn't.

"No you weren't. I can hear the wheels turning in your head."

"I'm not really worried about it. My mom knows and she is still willing to see me. I just remember what Jules said about stating a fact. I am really proud of you and of the life we've made together. We are both successful, it's not like I'm some diesel dyke who is sleeping with a crack whore." I was rationalizing out loud.

"Speaking of crack whores, how is your ex-girlfriend?" She giggled.

"Funny. It wasn't crack, it was pot. And I hear she got promoted to mail carrier."

"That's so much better than disease carrier."

"You want a black eye too?" I rolled over on top of her.

"You know Doc, it's gonna be okay. Twenty-four hours from now it will all be over. We will be back here in our bed together and they will be worrying about their flight to Spain."

"Unless I chicken out, then you will be bunking with Amelia."

"Hmmm," she smiled, "I hadn't thought of that."

"Careful, that's my new sister you're talking about."

Turkey Day had arrived. Not the actual holiday, but the house did smell like turkey by nine a.m. Its comforting aroma reminded me of the task at hand and I pulled my pillow over my head and tried to go back to sleep. No luck. The turkey made my stomach growl and I felt a little bit of excitement about sharing an "unofficial holiday" with my parents.

"Knock, knock!" A man's voice came from the door. I knew it was too early to be my father, so I assumed it was the chef. I pulled the covers up to my chin.

"Come in!" I hoped it was breakfast in bed time. I thought I smelled coffee. In walks a tray of pastries, coffee and juice. Carrying the tray was my big brother. "Jack! Holy shit! What are you doing here?"

"I was told that the parentals are coming and I was called in for backup."

"I would hug you but it seems that I am a bit on the nude side here."

"Hmm, please don't tell me that you sleep nude. What if your roommate sees you?"

"Oh. Jack, I'm gay. She's not my roommate, she's my partner."

"There, was that so hard? Now repeat it over and over for the next eight hours. Actually, I meant what if Amelia sees you? P.S., I know you're gay, you told me the day you married Steven."

"I don't care if Amelia sees me naked. I see her naked all the time."

Jack pretended to fall off the bed and fake a heart attack. "Oh, my gawd. Can I move in here too? Next you are gonna tell me that her friends come over and they have pillow fights."

"In your dreams. They come over and give each other massages. Oh, wait, that was in my dreams."

He pulled himself off the floor. "Okay, kitten. You go get dressed"—he kissed me on the cheek—"and for God's sake, brush your teeth. I'm gonna go watch your roommates swim."

"Can I ask you something before you go?"

"The answer is no, I am not gay too. Kidding. Ask me anything."

"Do you remember that snowstorm when we were kids?"

"Which one? It snowed seven months a year up there." He picked at a pastry.

"The one where it was so bad that you had to carry me home

from school."

"You exaggerate. I only carried you through the deep stuff. I do remember though."

"How come you carried me instead of Amy?"

"She didn't need to be carried. She was an independent kid. She would wear herself out before she let her dorky brother give her some help."

"Why do you suppose I let you help me?" I leaned back on my pillow.

"Don't know. You and I had a closer bond with each other than either one of us did with Amy. I felt a responsibility to take care of you both and keep an eye on my sisters. You just always seemed to need me and I liked being needed."

"Do you miss her?" I stared at the ceiling.

"I do miss her and I have regrets. I am glad that you were twins because I see things in you that remind me so much of her. Sometimes I feel like she is still here."

"I wish she was still here. Think she would have been okay with my life?"

"She adored you and would have adored anyone you brought home. She did know you were gay, Doc. She told me years ago that she knew it. She didn't have a problem with it. She was just annoyed that you didn't tell her outright. You did hint around a lot and she just hated that you held it in." He took my hand. I sat staring at the ceiling and tried to fight back tears.

"Let's not have regrets with each other." I took his other hand.

"Deal. And don't worry, I will always carry you through the deep stuff."

"Jack"—I almost cried again—"I'm really glad you're here. Sorry you had to miss work."

"I think the other mechanics can fix those cars for one day."

"Jack, you're a dentist."

"Oh, shit. If I've been fixing cars, who's been drilling teeth?" He winked and walked out.

• • •

The four of us swam for a few hours and made predictions about the evening's events. It was three to one that my dad would get drunk and my mom would spend the evening humming show tunes. I felt sure that I could go through with it and just wanted it to be over so we could enjoy the rest of my spring break. I knew that coming out would be much like Thanksgiving itself—days of preparation and it's over in five minutes with nothing left to do but clean it all up.

Jack went to the airport to surprise our parents while we three girls stayed behind to prepare. We sent the chef home, assuring him that we could handle carving the bird and burning the side dishes. He was not amused, but left anyway. Amelia disappeared to her room and the two of us fluffed pillows and straightened magazines.

"Hey, sweetie?" my helper smiled, "should the 'OUT' magazine go on top of 'The Advocate' or underneath it?"

"Oh, shit. We forgot to gay-proof the house."

"Are we gonna need to put those plastic things in the power outlets?" she mused.

"No, that's for kid-proofing. We need to make sure that there are not any plastic things that require power outlets."

We ran around in a frenzy looking for things that might be too revealing. I retrieved two Karin Kallmaker books and a framed photo of us with Melissa Etheridge. She came back with a music fest poster from Fire Island, an abstract nude oil painting, an Al Gore bumper sticker and a six-pack of Rolling Rock.

"Babe, aside from the poster, I think the rest is okay. My parents voted for Gore."

"Well, I wasn't sure if the painting said 'We love art' or 'We love boobies'."

"It's tasteful. We will let it say 'We love art' and on the inside we can think 'We love boobies'. Why the Rolling Rock?"

"Everyone knows that only gay people drink Rolling Rock."

"I'm gay and I didn't know that."

"Well, then let's just drink them anyway just in case your dad knows that."

"Okay, but only for the sake of hiding evidence."

We cracked open two beers and hid the other items in our closet. I thought of the irony of hiding my gayness in the closet after it took me so many years to get out of there. I decided not to overanalyze the obvious irony as we lay on the closet floor sipping our beers.

"Damn, I wish I had a cigarette." I sighed.

"Pot would be better. There is a pack of Marlboros in the freezer. You have time before you need to shower."

"Got any pot?" The thought of getting stoned sounded pretty good to me.

"Nope. You'll have to stick with nicotine."

I took the pack to the backyard and chain smoked three cigarettes. It was very relaxing, but I got such a head rush that I thought I was going to pass out. Our roommate came out and joined me. She lit us a cigarette and took a long drag.

"Has anyone ever told you that you look like Latin superstar Amelia Garcia?" I teased.

"I get that a lot. Has anyone ever told you that you look like a woman procrastinating?"

"Were you sent out here to retrieve me?"

"Yup. The party's over." She gave me a hound dog look.

"Tell me, superstar, got any advice for a woman who's fixin to disappoint her parents?"

"You're not going to disappoint them, Doc. You're merely going to throw them for a loop. I'm willing to bet that it will be okay." She took my hand. "I don't think anyone turns out exactly as their parents had hoped. I am sure my parents would have liked me to be a hotshot lawyer like the princess you live with. If my folks were still around, I am sure they would have hated the fact that I dance on stage half naked."

"Would you have pursued singing if your parents were around to try and stop you?"

"I would have pursued it. The passion I have for singing is inside me. I had to do something with it or I would have been miserable. It's a little like your being gay—it is part of who you are and no one can stop your passion. If Mama and Papa were around, they would have discouraged me but if I showed them how happy it made me, they would have understood and maybe even joined me on tour."

"So you think my parents will understand and maybe even love her like their own daughter?"

"I don't know for sure because I don't know them. I would like to think that the world is perfect and that we can all just get along. I know that people have their own opinions and their own shortcomings. I know that I love both of you like you are my own sisters and no matter what happens with your parents, you still have family."

"Thanks, Amelia. You are a great sister and you would have made an excellent lawyer."

"Thanks, Doc. You are a great sister too, but you're too smart to be a lawyer."

I flicked my last butt over the fence and gathered up my beer, lighter and Marlboros.

"You can leave those," she pointed at the pack.

"I thought you didn't smoke." I worried about her voice.

"I thought you didn't smoke either."

I went in the house and checked on the turkey—still a ways to go. I sampled some of the stuffing and made my way to the shower. Girlie girl was blow drying her hair.

"Jack called. The plane is a little late, they should be here in an hour though."

"So I had time to chain smoke a few more?" I didn't need the head rush.

"No, you need to get dressed and help me in the kitchen. I laid out some clothes on the bed for you. I really hope you weren't planning on wearing that awful silk blouse your mom sent you."

"No, my navel ring pokes through the fabric. One confession at a time. What are you going to wear when you meet your in-laws for the first time?"

"You know, I never thought about them like that. Great, thanks, now I'm nervous. I am wearing jeans and a white shirt."

"Very nice. White is so pure and innocent." I walked to the bed to see what she had picked out for me. I found a vintage cowboy shirt, faded Levi's, boots and sandals. "Hey, where did all this come from?"

"I told you we spent the day shopping yesterday while you were busy being a Stepford wife."

"I love the shirt and the boots are awesome, better than the sandals even. But I planned on going a different route, maybe a little more femme."

"Babe, you still look femme in snap shirts. Just be comfortable, remember, you are who you are."

"Who am I again? All the cleaning and cooking has made me forget."

"Who are you? Hmmm." She looked pensive. "You are an Aerosmith, Warhol, Parker-loving college professor hot lesbian with great legs and an amazing sense of style. Who am I?"

"You, madam, are a fantastic partner who is so getting laid tomorrow." I grinned.

She helped me slip into my jeans and boots and loaned me her diamond earrings. Ready or not, here I come (out).

Just as I was basting the bird and fighting off the cat, I heard Jack's knock at the front door. We'd had the same knock since we were kids—very unmistakable—*tap tika tika tap tap*. Every inch of my body went numb and I felt a cool wave of nausea rush to my stomach. It turned to my partner, looking for strength. She was white as a sheet and her hands were shaking.

"Is it too late to run?" my voice squeaked.

"Just relax and get the door." She was in worse shape than me.

"You get the door, I'm cooking."

"They're your parents, you get the door."

"I'll give you a dollar if you get it." I reached into my empty pocket.

"Jeeeezus! I'll get the damn door!" Amelia left the kitchen in a huff.

We heard muted voices from the entryway, an exchange of pleasantries. I was relieved that my parents recognized Amelia but didn't gush. Both of us froze as footsteps approached the kitchen. I felt like I was back in high school and was about to get caught with a girl in my bed. We took one last look at each other and I suddenly found the strength I needed to get through this. I remembered why I needed to do this and the reason for my existence was the woman standing in front of me. Suddenly nothing mattered and I almost shouted it out the minute I saw my dad. "I'm gay and this is my life partner! We are getting married in Holland and you can't come because you are an ass and you smell like static!" Instead, I put on my best daughter behavior.

"Hi, Mom. You look great!" Big awkward hug, no kiss. "Dad, good to see you!" Amazingly, awkward kiss with no hug. Some things never change.

I wasn't sure how to introduce my partner, so I didn't. Jack stepped in and did the intros. He was very casual about the whole thing and never committed to the word "roommate." I was pleased and grateful. He shot me a wink that reminded me of the first time I realized that he suspected I was gay. We both eyed the same blonde at the movie theater and as we checked her out head to toe, she smiled at me, and Jack shot me that wonderful wink.

"Drinks, who would like a drink?" I walked toward the bar.

My mom checked her watch, "Oh my, it's too early for anything harsh. I'll just have a Shirley Temple." You could tell she wanted tequila shooters and a beer back.

"A cherry Sprite for mom. Dad, what can I get you?" I already knew the answer.

"Bar water for me." He didn't bother to check his watch.

"Well, we are on vacation. Make mine a screwdriver instead." My mom blushed.

I suddenly wanted to ram a screwdriver into her head and I don't know why. I think I resented the Midwestern Pollyanna routine.

I mixed the drinks for my folks and poured a pitcher from the keg for us young 'uns. We gathered on the patio and sipped our drinks listening to the vacation itinerary and tales from the small town. Amelia was fascinated by their lifestyle and they were quite taken by her presence. I stayed silent and I realized that I had nothing in common with anybody. I wasn't a cowgirl, I wasn't a lawyer or a superstar or even a dentist. I was an eccentric nerd who preferred cheap beer to expensive chardonnay. I felt like such an ass when I realized that I was too good for my own family and not good enough for the Laine family. I deserved to be alone in the closet and decided I should distance myself from all these people immediately.

I finished off the pitcher and started in on another. My partner gave me that "slow down" look that we have mastered at parties over the years. I ignored her and poured another glass.

"Dinner will be at least another hour, anyone for swimming?"

My partner choked on her appetizer. "What about your, um, sunburn?"

"You only live once, lady," I beamed and she grinned back in awe.

I returned from the house ten minutes later wearing a bikini top and swim trunks. I was prepared for the interrogation and one immediately ensued.

"Is that a ring in your navel?" Jack the smart ass had to start the ball rolling.

I smiled and nodded.

My mom looked deflated, "Aren't you a little old. You should know better."

"You're only as old as you feel." I dove into the deep end.

My dad came out of the house wearing tight trunks tucked under his hairy beer belly. He dove into the pool behind me and swam toward the spa. I was waiting for my mom to tell him I had a navel ring when I noticed a blue streak on my dad's back. I swam toward him to get a closer look. I about choked on the water when I realized that he had a tattoo. I really freaked when I realized that it was the same infinity tattoo as mine in almost the same location on my shoulder blade. I felt elated and nauseated at the same time. Finally I had a connection to my father but did it make the rebel in me less of a rebel?

"Alfred, your daughter has a navel ring." Her tone was spiteful.

"She does? How about that? Did it hurt, kid?"

"Nah, only when it got infected." I was hoping to get a rise.

We swam in unison for a few minutes when Amelia broke the silence. "Hey, you guys have the same tattoo. Did you go together?"

"I got mine in New York about twenty-five years ago. I didn't know she even had one."

"I didn't know you had one either, Dad."

"Sure you knew. You used to trace its outline through my white T-shirts."

It suddenly became clear to me why I had to have that exact design. Everyone was trying to talk me into a gay flag or a peace sign. I had to have the infinity. My mind must have blocked the memory of my dad's tattoo and my affection toward it. I dove under water to recover from the shock. My plan of showing my independence had backfired and everyone was okay. I felt that the next bomb might drop well. I was ready for dinner.

The table was a masterpiece. The new china and crystal

complemented the amazing silver and linens. I pretended that I had picked it all out over the years. I didn't feel the need to explain that a designer spent thousands of dollars less than two days ago. With all six of us working together, we managed to get all the food out of the ovens and onto platters. It looked better than Thanksgiving and I had a sudden urge to watch football.

We had the obligatory "Where is Steven?" conversation. I blew it off and forced myself to remain calm when they reminded me what a shame it was that we divorced. We talked about the Laine Hotel and her career as a lawyer. Jack told us in too much detail about his worst patients. Amelia was quiet and laughed politely. You could tell she was missing Tobias. I was too. Everyone devoured their gourmet turkey and went back for seconds. I picked at my plate, wishing I could just order a pizza and go to bed. Someone was kicking me under the table and I looked around for the culprit. When my eyes met Jack's he mouthed the words "Do it, Dorko." I glanced at my mate and her steel blue eyes told me it was time to say something. She had been wonderful all day and seemed to enjoy my family as much as I did hers. I knew I had to make her a member of mine the way she did for me. My heart raced and my hands shook. I finished my glass of wine and leaned toward my parents.

"I need to tell you something. I want you to know that I am healthy and very happy in my life. I want you to know that I have found love and that I am loved in return. I want you to know that I am gay and . . ."

I stopped talking when I saw my dad's face. I had no idea what to do. I couldn't tell if he was choking on my words or on the green beans. Yup, it was the beans. Jack swooped up my father and administered the Heimlich. The hunk of bean shot from my dad's mouth onto the pumpkin pie. We all stared at the man, waiting for him to speak.

"That pie is mine." He started laughing and reached for the dish.

"Dad, did you hear what I said?" I didn't want to repeat it.

"You said you are happy."

"That's not all I said, Dad."

"Well, that's all I need to hear. Your mom's the one who's gonna be a pain in the ass about this. I don't care if you are a gay ax murderer as long as you are happy and as long as you give me some of this pie." He dug his fingers into the green bean and pumpkin combo.

"Alfred, I don't think you understand. She is sleeping in the same bed as her roommate."

"Which one, the rich lawyer or the rich singer? Either way she has my approval."

"She sleeps with me. We share a life together." The lawyer spoke.

"Be good to her, she's a good kid." He looked proud.

"Yes sir, she is a good kid and I try to be very good to her."

My mom pushed her plate away and stood. "I've had enough of this politeness. You corrupted my child with your money and your lifestyle. You probably broke up her marriage. Poor Steven." She stormed from the room and none of us moved.

"Someone should go after her," my mate said, reaching for the wine bottle.

"You go, I'm eating." I said with a mouthful.

"You go, she's your mother," my mate insisted.

"I'll give you a dollar to go after her." I reached into my empty pocket.

"Jeeeezus! I'll go!" Amelia went running after my mom in a huff.

The rest of us sat and drank and discussed our plans for Amsterdam.

Amelia managed to get my mom calmed down by sending her to the Laine for the night. She refused to sleep in our house knowing that we would be in the same bed. She refused to go home with Jack since he was on our side. She was furious with my father's attitude and promised to make the plane ride to Spain a living hell. What irked me is that she knew I was gay when she came here. She never said a word about not sleeping in our home. I found it ironic that she had no problem getting a free room at the hotel or a ride in the limo compliments of the woman who corrupted me. I think she was really counting on my dad being upset about the situation. She planned to just be the martyr who stands by her man despite her own opinion. The fact that he was okay with it really pissed her off and ruined her plan. I suspected my dad truly was upset but he would never cause a scene in front of strangers. I decided to ignore both of their responses until things had a chance to sink in a bit.

After a few rounds of poker and too many drinks, we all headed off to bed. Jack tried, to no avail, to bunk with Amelia. She said she was flattered but dentists gave her nightmares. I tried calling my mom at the hotel, but a do not disturb block was placed on her phone.

"You asleep?" I shook her abruptly.

"Not any more, jackass."

"How do you think it went?"

She was quiet for a minute, "I think they will both need time to adapt. They will go through all the steps but in the long run, they will both be fine."

"Yeah. I can't wait till happy hour so we can tell the girls what happened. I came out to my parents. My dad got a bean stuck in his throat, my mom got one stuck in her ass."

"Go to sleep, you big freak."

"I love you."

"I love you more."

Chapter Eighteen

We had a very awkward brunch at the hotel before returning my parents to the airport. Their minds were on the trip ahead. I knew they would worry about me when they returned. My mom seemed better about things the next morning. I mentioned that a good night's sleep always helps. She said that she met the nicest couple in the bar named Arthur and Anna. Apparently they also have a gay daughter and helped my mom understand a few things. I was shocked to later learn that Amelia had actually called them and set up the whole encounter. I was even more shocked to learn that the Laines were on my side.

We left Amelia at the hotel since there was a chance that Tobias would get back in a day or two. We debated whether we would go ahead and fly to Vegas or just take it easy for the remaining five days of our break.

"Ever feel like we have been running nonstop since you moved in?" I was tired.

"Yeah, it's a real roller coaster, one thing after another. Kinda like a bad lesbian novel."

I had to laugh, "Well, except neither one of us has gotten sick or died."

"There are still loose ends and years to go, you never know."

I took her hand as we headed down our street toward the house. After much discussion, we decided not to go to Vegas but rather to stay home and enjoy the fact that our house was finally a home. We took the time to appreciate each and every room and painted a wall or two. I spent some time writing and painting a canvas I figured I would never finish. The cat seemed confused with our constant presence. He finally hid under the bed for two days searching for some privacy. I spent some time searching for what I wanted to do with my life. I was happy at the university but I had no desire to go beyond my current position. As much as I wanted to chuck it all and take a year off to write, I felt weird about asking for the financial support. I also knew I would go crazy if I didn't have a fixed routine and daily drive. I needed a constant, and relying on my own mind for distraction would never work. I wasn't sure what I needed to do to find the answers but I knew continuous excitement, drinking and stress was not the answer.

"Doc, you want to drive up to Splinter's for some pool?"

"Can we stay someplace close? I don't want to drive that far."

"We can take the new truck. It's a nice night for it."

"Babe, I don't know what I want to do. Let's just stay in."

"Let's compromise, we'll go to The Attic and see a bad band. During intermission, you can tell me why you are so wishy-washy. If your student is bartending, we will leave."

"Deal."

We dressed with little interest to the wardrobe. It was nice to throw on a hat and jeans for once without worrying about a formal occasion or that Amelia's press would be stalking us. The bar was clear of students, which made sense since most were probably in Padre dancing naked on the beach for the break. We ordered a couple of cokes and split a plate of nachos.

"What's up, Doc? Why the long face?"

"I think it all just caught up with me, the families, the wedding plans, all of it. I just have no idea what the future holds."

"Isn't that the fun part of it? Life is full of surprises, life is good."

"It's good for you. You love being a lawyer, you are new to your career, it's all still exciting for you. I have been teaching since you were still in high school. Its tired."

"I hate it when you remind me how young I am."

"I feel old, babe. You all have great lives, I am in a redundant cycle. Amelia has her fame and new husband. You have the glamorous family and hotels. Toby gets to travel the world, Jack loves being a dentist, Steven has a kid. I feel like I am going nowhere riding on ya'll's coattails."

"You could travel the world if you want. You could go to medical school, you could even take singing lessons. You make it seem like it's all over for you, like you are some shriveled up old lady who never amounted to anything. What about having a kid? Do you still want to be a mommy?"

"I do want to have a baby with you but I feel like I need to do something for myself first. Like I said the night of Toby and Amelia's reception, there are so many things I still want to do. I feel like I have not made an impact and if we jump into parenthood, I will spend the next eighteen years with no identity of my own. I will always be *partner* or *mom,* or *the lady who used to teach*. I want to have something of my own. I just can't figure out what it is."

"Well, Doc, there is no doubt in my mind that you will figure it out and whatever it is, you will be brilliant at it."

"I appreciate that. So it's okay to put off the baby plans for a bit?"

"Of course it's okay. I will tell Toby to put the sperm back on ice and I will call off the baby shower. I figured we should enjoy some things alone first anyway. I mean, my goodness, woman, we haven't even lived together for a year yet."

We sat and watched the band. My heart rate returned to normal and I thought the panic of my future had finally subsided. I relaxed and actually started having fun—good sober fun with a bad band, no superstars and no worries. The bar grew so crowded that I couldn't get the waitress's attention. I went up to the bar to pay our check and ran into a familiar face. Something was different about this face since the last time I saw it. It was clean and smiling.

"Olympia? Is that you?"

"Hey, professor. Whassup?"

"Olympia, didn't I see you like a week ago and you were in total despair? Now you are here looking as shiny as a new nickel and drinking with friends?"

"Ah, sorry about the sob story that night. What can I say, I'm young. One minute your world is coming to an end and the next, everything is peachy. I am staying with a friend who got me a job at a video store. Things were never really that bad. Ever notice how your own problems seem really big?"

"That's because they are happening to you. I'm glad you're okay."

"Thanks. Are you okay?" She actually seemed interested.

"I am okay, just trying to figure out what to do with my life."

"Well, Professor, looks like you've done pretty good so far from what I saw last week. You're a good teacher and a good person. Just do what makes you happy."

"It's figuring out what makes you happy that's the hard part." I sighed.

"Then just figure out what doesn't make you happy and don't do it."

"Is it that easy? Sometimes you have to do things that don't make you happy in order to survive." I realized I was searching for answers from a stranger.

"Like I said, I'm young. What do I know about life?"

"I'm guessing you know more than most."

She just smiled and gave me a hug. I met my partner outside and we embarked on the short walk home.

"Wasn't that the homeless girl you were talking to?"

"Not homeless any more. Sounds like she got her life in order."

"In a week? Wow, I bet you're jealous. Did she give you all the answers?"

"No, but she gave me the right questions."

I lay in bed that night thinking about all the people in my life, all the choices I had made and all the things I had yet to do. I realized that I did have a great life, a life many people would kill for. I thought about my past and realized that like Olympia, I was young once. The problem with my youth was that I did do the things that didn't make me happy. I played the straight role and got married. I rushed into a career at which I was very successful but it was too stressful too soon. I thought about the fact that I hid my lifestyle from people who loved me, knowing deep down inside that who I am mattered more than who I was expected to be.

I thought about my career and my students. I loved being an educator and felt that I made a difference to some people. I loved having the opportunity to share my passion for literature with my students. I loved having a captive audience to whom I could make jokes or give advice. I loved the university itself with all its history and energy. It was so inspiring to be a part of something so big and important. On the other hand, I perhaps took it a little too seriously. The redundancy of teaching had started wearing on me over the last year. I wasn't sure how many more times I could give a dazzling lecture on the same books over and over. I wasn't sure how many more times I could make that long drive ten times a week. Twenty-five hundred miles a month was a lot for anyone. I always dreamed of sleeping past seven and working from my own home. I dreamed of being the writer the lectures were about, not the lecturer herself. I went to college to be a writer and somewhere along the way I got realistic and decided that teaching was a noble profession. If I no longer felt noble, maybe I should go back to my roots and start over. Maybe I should take advantage of my situation and opportunities and give it a college try.

I thought about Amy, my twin, my greatest sorrow. I wondered what she would have done with her life if she didn't get cancer. I wondered if she would have been proud of me. I wished I had more time to love her and I wished I had taken more time to grieve. I thought about my amazing brother Jack and promised that I would not take my surviving sibling for granted. I wondered if he missed Amy as much as I did and I wondered why he and I never talked about her anymore. I thought about the role that Steven played in my life. He was the true definition of a man, he loved me like a princess and let me go to find my own kingdom. I realized that I needed to let go of him, that we both needed to get on with our lives.

The crushing weight in my thoughts that night was my parents. My mom's initial reaction on the phone was so much more accepting that her response in person. I decided that *seeing* my life was a bit more sobering to her than just hearing about it. If they had suspected for so many years that I was gay, why didn't they ask me? Didn't they realize that one awkward moment in high school would have been so much better than the anguish of my twenties? I wondered if they would come around or if I had to write them off like so many other people who hated me for being gay. I was fooled by my father's reaction and was mad at myself for that. He seemed okay at dinner, but afterward he became quiet and distant. I should have known that he would never be okay with anything I did. I decided to let them come to me, that I would not chase down their approval, I would not play their game. They would come around.

I thought about the Laine family. I was always jealous of the way they all got along. They had no expectations of each other. They took everything on its face and with all the money in the world, they were just good, down-to-earth people. Arthur and Anna loved their children so much that lifestyle choices never mattered. They were the definition of class in every sense of the word. Tobias and Amelia were in love but they had a kind of love that meant they lived their own lives and saw each other when they had time. I had a hard time understanding that—I could never spend more than a few nights away from my true love. I was envious that Toby and Amelia could be married legally and never had to hide their relationship. Like most straight people, I think they took some things for granted.

I thought about my amazing and beautiful life partner. My inspiration. I didn't have any worries or questions when it came to her. I knew where we stood at all times, I loved and felt the same love in return. I waited my whole life for someone I trusted enough to let me be me. She was so much more than I ever imagined, than I ever deserved. I admired her for so many things, mainly because of the way the world looked though her eyes, the way I looked through her eyes. She was my future. No matter what I decided to do with my life, there was no doubt that she would be by my side. It was then that I realized that she was my muse, and I knew what I had to do with my life.

I quietly crawled out of bed and stumbled across the house to the office. I booted up my computer and started a pot of coffee. With my first cup in hand I sat behind my computer, ready to change my life. Just as I began typing, I heard a light tap on the door.

"You okay, Doc?"

"Yeah, baby. I'm fine. Go back to bed."

"Okay, let me know if you need me."

"I do need you, Sam. I know what I need to do for me and if I fall, I need you to pick me up." I almost started crying, I think I was scared to tell her what I decided to do.

"I got you, you got me, we got each other. What are you gonna do?"

"I'm gonna write a book."

"It's about time. What are you gonna write about?"

"The only thing I am passionate about. I am gonna write about us."

She stared at me for a minute then nodded her head and smiled as she closed the door. I settled back in and began my journey:

Untitled
By Dani O'Connor (D.O.C.)

My Internet profile read like this:

Educated MTV addict with a penchant for bad fashion and dull conversation seeks overly attractive, high maintenance, money grubbing, curious, "straight" woman for bad dates and awkward kisses. You should be prepared to use me anytime and dump me on a whim to return to your husband/boyfriend. I am into transcendental vegetation . . . "I think, therefore, I yam." I like long walks through airports and singing in public restrooms. I have perfect teeth and perfect feet. Everything in between is a cruel joke told by gravity. I am in a very vulnerable place in my life, so please be willing to take advantage of my insecurities and need for affection. I drink, smoke and use prescription medication. You should be prepared to overlook my chain-smoking, drug addiction and alcoholism; but feel free to complain about it every second of every date. I do not have a sense of humor and I lack patience. If I tell you that you are a flake, I am being serious. Please do not laugh at everything I say, as I am sure most of the time it will go over your head. Boring tales of your job will put me to sleep. I need sleep, so please don't try to wake me. Any attempt to change my hair, clothes or habits will lead to bitter resentment and removal from my Christmas card list. You must insist on flaunting me in front of all your exes and treat me like dirt when they don't respond. More important, you must treat me like less than dirt if they do respond. Please don't invite me to the wedding; getting you back together is reward enough. I don't like intellectual conversation, so I would appreciate a woman who is not familiar with Darwin, Dorothy Parker or anyone not associated with "Cosmo" magazine. I am turned on by women who call me "hun" and use alternate spellings like "kewl." If you think you can meet any or all of my criteria, I would love to hear from you. Normal, intelligent, funny, fit, attractive women need not apply; you don't exist. I might as well date the Easter Bunny.

Publications from Spinsters Ink

P.O. Box 242

Midway, Florida 32343
Phone: 800-301-6860
www.spinstersink.com

DISORDERLY ATTACHMENTS by Jennifer L. Jordan. 5th Kristin Ashe Mystery. Kris investigates whether a mansion someone wants to convert into condos is haunted. ISBN 1-883523-74-5 $14.95

VERA'S STILL POINT by Ruth Perkinson. Vera is reminded of exactly what it is that she has been missing in life.
ISBN 1-883523-73-7 $14.95

OUTRAGEOUS by Sheila Ortiz-Taylor. Arden Benbow, a motorcycle riding, lesbian Latina poet from LA is hired to teach poetry in a small liberal arts college in northwest Florida.
ISBN 1-883523-72-9 $14.95

UNBREAKABLE by Blayne Cooper. The bonds of love and friendship can be as strong as steel. But are they unbreakable?
ISBN 1-883523-76-1 $14.95

ALL BETS OFF by Jaime Clevenger. Bette Lawrence is about to find out how hard life can be for someone of low society standing in the 1900s. ISBN 1-883523-71-0 $14.95

UNBEARABLE LOSSES by Jennifer L. Jordan. 4th in the Kristin Ashe Mystery series. Two elderly sisters have hired Kris to discover who is pilfering from their award-winning holiday display.
ISBN 1-883523-68-0 $14.95

FRENCH POSTCARDS by Jane Merchant. When Elinor moves to France with her husband and two children, she never expects that her life is about to be changed forever.

ISBN 1-883523-67-2 $14.95

EXISTING SOLUTIONS by Jennifer L. Jordan. 2nd book in the Kristin Ashe Mystery series. When Kris is hired to find an activist's biological father, things get complicated when she finds herself falling for her client. ISBN 1-883523-69-9 $14.95

A SAFE PLACE TO SLEEP by Jennifer L. Jordan. 1st in the Kristin Ashe Mystery series. Kris is approached by well known lesbian Destiny Greaves with an unusual request. One that will lead Kris to hunt for her own missing childhood pieces.

ISBN 1-883523-70-2 $14.95

THE SECRET KEEPING by Francine Saint Marie. The Secret Keeping is a high stakes, girl-gets-girl romance, where the moral of the story is that money can buy you love if it's invested wisely.

ISBN: 1-883523-77-X $14.95

WOMEN'S STUDIES by Julia Watts. With humor and heart, Women's Studies follows one school year in the lives of these three young women and shows than in college, one's extracurricular activities are often much more educational that what goes on in the classroom. ISBN: 1-883523-75-3 $14.95

A POEM FOR WHAT'S HER NAME by Dani O'Connor. Professor Dani O'Connor had pretty much resigned herself to the fact that there was no such thing as a complete woman. Then out of nowhere, along comes a woman who blows Dani's theory right out of the water. ISBN: 1-883523-78-8 $14.95